Red Cap

G. Clifton Wisler

PUFFIN BOOKS

PUFFIN BOOKS

Published by the Penguin Group

Penguin Books USA Inc., 375 Hudson Street, New York, New York 10014, U.S.A.

Penguin Books Ltd, 27 Wrights Lane, London W8 5TZ, England

Penguin Books Australia Ltd, Ringwood, Victoria, Australia

Penguin Books Canada Ltd, 10 Alcorn Avenue, Toronto, Ontario, Canada M4V 3B2

Penguin Books (N.Z.) Ltd, 182-190 Wairau Road, Auckland 10, New Zealand

Penguin Books Ltd, Registered Offices: Harmondsworth, Middlesex, England

First published in the United States of America by Lodestar Books,
an affiliate of Dutton Children's Books, a division of Penguin Books USA Inc., 1991
Published in Puffin Books, 1994

23 24 25 26 27 28 29 30

THE LIBRARY OF CONGRESS HAS CATALOGED THE LODESTAR BOOKS EDITION AS FOLLOWS:
Wisler, G. Clifton.
Red Cap / G. Clifton Wisler. p. cm.
Summary: A young Yankee drummer boy displays great courage
when he's captured and sent to Andersonville Prison.
ISBN 0-525-67337-7
1. Powell, Ransom J. 1849-1899—Juvenile fiction.
2. United States—History—Civil War, 1861-1865—Prisoners and
prisons, Confederate—Juvenile fiction. 3. Andersonville Prison—
Juvenile fiction. [1. Powell, Ransom J., 1849-1899—Fiction.
2. United States—History—Civil War, 1861-1865—
Prisoners and prisons—Fiction. 3. Andersonville Prison—Fiction.] I. Title.
PZ7.W78033Re 1991 [Fic]—dc20 90-21944 CIP AC

Puffin Books ISBN 0-14-036936-8

Printed in the United States of America

In memory of
RANSOM J. POWELL
(1849–1899)
private and drummer
Company I, 10th West Virginia
Volunteer Infantry

"No six-footer had a more soldierly heart than little Red Cap, and none was more loyal to the cause. He was, beyond a doubt, the best known and most popular person in the prison."

—John McElroy
16th Illinois Cavalry

Red Cap

1

I was born and reared in the little town of Frostburg, Maryland, way out west from Baltimore in Allegheny County. That was mining country, and most boys by the time they had half their growth would be digging coal and coughing dust. I guess you'd say I was lucky, all things considered, as my pa was Frostburg's blacksmith and we did passable well.

"I won't have my eldest scratching coal from these hills," Pa told Mr. Havers, the schoolmaster, one day when he thought I was out of hearing. "Ransom's quick. Does my accounts already, and he's not much past twelve."

"And frail for a miner," Mr. Havers agreed. "Smallish. But just let the other boys have at him! They find him game, James. No shortage of fortitude to him. He writes a fair hand, too, and he's read through the library. I have to send to Cumberland for books. He puts the others to shame."

I took that as high praise, for neither Pa nor Mr. Havers was long on compliments. To me they might complain of laziness or chastise a bit of devilment. I saw through it, though, noting the grins and nodding heads. To hear Grandpa Powell tell it, Pa himself was good at raising old Harry. And Mr. Havers wasn't past wrestling with the older boys when the occasion presented itself.

So you see I didn't go to the army an orphan, or unwanted, as many a boy did in those days. No, and it wasn't on account of strong politics. Who knew much about such things as a child? Truth is, war caught most of us kind of sideways, by surprise. Was about the middle of April 1861, and Mr. Havers called us to order.

"You all know there's been talk of breaking apart the Union," he told us. "Half the southern states have joined in a confederacy. The hotheads down in South Carolina have fired on the flag. They've shelled Fort Sumter, in Charleston harbor, and taken the place by force of arms. So you see, boys and girls, there will be a war."

That was mighty perplexing. I had a hard time understanding why what Carolinians did with Charleston forts had much to do with us up in Maryland. I wasn't alone. That afternoon, when we were let out of the schoolhouse, I followed Oliver Wilson and Enos Perkins out to the Perkins farm. It had turned to hot, and we three being the eldest males still devoted to education in Frostburg, it was just natural we formed a company of sorts at such times. The Perkins place wasn't a mile outside of town, and they had a fine deep pond perfect for swimming off the springtime wearies.

"Ransom, aren't you coming home?" my sister Mary, who was ten, called. Nancy, who was two years younger, added her usual echo.

"Going out to the Perkins place," I told them.

"You'll be late for chores," Mary warned.

"Been late before," I told them. "Now shoo!"

Mary and Nancy dogged my heels, and I turned in a rush. It was hard to put much scare into those two. Mary was as tall as I was, and she was a natural busybody. Nancy was her shadow.

"I told you to shoo!" I hollered. Ollie and Enos, each of them half a head taller than I and showing signs of whiskering, hugged my flanks. The three of us were in no mood to be followed. Heavy things were brewing down south, and we had words to swap.

"Ranse, Pa said you—" Mary began. Ollie reached over, grabbed her slate, and tossed it toward a watering trough twenty feet away. Nancy vanished, and Mary, reading the threat of much worse to come in my fiery eyes, prudently retreated.

"Let's go 'fore somebody else takes after us," Ollie urged, and the three of us lit out for the farm.

Half an hour later we were splashing around in the shallows, near drowning each other like we'd been doing since we were small fry. It was about then that Enos's brother Patrick happened by, sweat-streaked from breaking ground and looking for a bit of foolishness. Wasn't anytime before Pat joined the fun, with us three littler ones doing our best to haul him into deep water. He fended us off like a big brown bear, which he pretty much was, all tall and sporting a hairy chin.

It was later, when we'd worn ourselves out, that Pat asked Enos for news.

"It's out and out war," Enos explained. "Fort Sumter."

"Figured somethin' big to have happened," Pat remarked with a shake of his shaggy hair. "Was a fellow by this mornin' talkin' secession."

"By Maryland?" Ollie asked. "We got no slaves to fight over."

"Plenty of 'em in the state," Pat pointed out. "They still got auctions in Baltimore, you know."

"My Uncle Gabe down in Fairfax County, Virginia, has twenty, thirty hands," Enos reminded us. "Says that gorilla Lincoln's got no business tellin' him what he can do with 'em."

"Isn't right, ownin' other folks," Ollie declared. His pa was a preacher and a bit of an abolitionist. The words just sort of leaked out, but they ignited our own little war right there at the pond. Next thing I knew Ollie and Enos were wrestling in the grass, rolling here and there, whacking elbows against foreheads, kicking and walloping. Pat had a try at pulling 'em apart and got a lump on his jaw for the trouble. Me, I wasn't sixty pounds in boots and britches, and I had neither on at that moment. Finally Ollie got a knee in his belly, and the air rushed out, leaving him blue as summer sky.

"Ollie, I didn't mean nothin'," Enos said as he and I tried to get our friend's lungs to working again. Wasn't much that hurt as bad as getting the wind kneed out of you.

"Know that," Ollie finally muttered as he got his breath.

We stared at one another, all solemn and still. I guess that's when we knew Mr. Havers was right about there coming a war. If we took to blows over things, being the best of friends since any of us could walk, then older folks sure weren't above firing off cannons and marching regiments against each other.

"Maybe we ought to go along home," I suggested as I collected my clothes. "I got chores, after all."

"I need to help Pa wash the church windows," Ollie

4

added. "Guess you got eggs to gather or something, eh, Enos?"

"He can help me pack," Pat told us. "I'm bound south. Been on my mind a while, and now with shootin', I'll be joinin' Uncle Gabe's company. First Virginia Cavalry."

"Virginia's not joined all this foolishness, has she?" Ollie asked.

The Perkins boys chafed at Ollie's words, but they held their tongues.

"Won't be long now till Gorilla Abe calls for troops," Pat explained. "Southern rights bind Virginia to her neighbors."

"Maryland's sure to come along, too," Enos added. "Watch and see."

I gazed at Ollie, who was shaking his head. Neither of us spoke. Instead we climbed into our clothes and headed to town with only a wave of farewell to send Pat on his way.

That was the last time I saw Patrick Perkins.

We didn't see much of Enos, either. He took over the plowing, and that kept him busy. He didn't come to school. And when Ollie and I walked out to the pond, we didn't feel welcome.

"Things've changed," I told Ollie. "Look around Frostburg. You don't see many men these days. I hear the mines've lost half their diggers."

"Gone to fight for the Union," Ollie told me. "A few've headed south."

After President Lincoln called for volunteers to fight the rebels, as he termed the southern states, Virginia pulled out of the Union. A few other states voted secession, too, but not Maryland. A batch of Baltimore planters formed some reb regiments, but the state legislature voted fifty-three to thirteen against leaving. Feelings around Frostburg, where folks dug coal or plowed fields for themselves, were pretty one sided.

"Rally to the colors, friends," one bewhiskered colonel urged when he came to town enlisting for his regiment. "We'll make short work of this rebellion. Be back home for harvest."

"Bunch of fools," Pa told me as we walked home after the speechifying. "Go get their idiot heads shot off. Can't a one of them remember Mexico."

I wasn't all that unhappy Pa was staying home. He had Ma, the girls, my tiny brother Jamie, and me to worry after. One apprentice, too—Johnny McDonald, who, though only a year older than I, was muscled and tall.

"You figured out what it's all about, Pa?" I asked him when we sat beside the forge later that night.

"Oh, everybody's got his version," Pa answered. "South wants to have its own way on slavery. On trade. Some say it's the farmers battling the factory people. I don't know. I've never held with slaveholding, Ranse. But it does seem like those people ought to make the choice themselves."

"I only ever met one slave," I whispered. "Caesar."

"That was last summer," Pa said, frowning.

He recalled it, too. Was a dandy up from Georgia come to reclaim this runaway caught in Pennsylvania. Caesar wasn't any older than Pat Perkins, but trouble had aged him. His hard black back was crisscrossed with red lines left by a lash, and his owner had cut off two fingers for his running away.

"I don't see a man's got rights to mutilate another," Pa had grumbled even while he'd made shackles for the Georgian. Business was business, after all.

"Hurt much?" I'd asked Caesar later when I'd brought him some food and water. He'd been holding his mangled hand sort of gingerly, and his eyes were red.

"Some," Caesar had confessed. "They some of 'em cuts a man's feets. Fingers ain't so bad."

"Was it worth it, though?"

"Worth it?" he'd asked, laughing. "Boy who's been free all his life ask me that? I been a slave seventeen years. Was free six months. Yeah, it were worth it. I give the whole hand for a year."

When I'd shared that story with Ollie's Pa, Pastor Wilson had turned pale.

"There'll come a day of retribution," he had promised. "Recompense for the wicked."

Other colonels rode into Frostburg as summer commenced. Each one urged the men to sign the muster book and put down the rebellion, and week by week the male population of Allegheny County shrank. Was about then that I escaped from the forge long enough to visit Enos at his farm.

"Go ahead and have a swim, son," Mr. Perkins said when I found Enos in the fields. "It's hot enough."

"I got my work," Enos objected. But his father waved us along, and I gladly led the way. As we kicked off our shoes and slipped out of our overalls, Enos gazed my way and rubbed his eyes.

I knew right off something had happened.

"Pat's got himself killed at a place called Culpepper," Enos told me.

"That's hard news," I said, swallowing a shudder.

"I aim to take his place," Enos added. "Uncle Gabe's got a

7

spot for me. First Virginia. They ride with Jeb Stuart, you know. Might take you, too, Ranse. Want to come?"

I did and I didn't. Was adventure calling, and it had a hard pull to it.

"I never rode a horse except to Cumberland," I finally said. "Then my feet couldn't find the stirrups. I'm not big enough for a soldier, folks say."

"Be harder to shoot," he told me. "I'll be wantin' company, Ranse. Hard times, Pat said in his letters. Uncle Gabe'd welcome you, and I can teach you to ride."

"Pa'd raise old Harry," I explained.

"Oh, you never pay him all that much mind. He's got that McDonald boy to help at the forge. What say? Ride with the First?"

"Can't," I told him.

"It's all that talk of Ollie's, isn't it?" he asked. "You don't hold with the cause."

"I don't," I confessed, realizing it myself for the first time.

"Then you ought to join the Blue, curse 'em. You and Ollie both. Instead you sit back and hide like a girl from your duty. That's the way of the North. I thought Marylanders came with stiffer backbones. Guess not."

"Don't figure we'll be swimming," I said, stepping back into my overalls. "Nor me staying. Wouldn't want to remember us parting with blows, Enos. We been friends too long."

"A friend'd ride south with me," he argued. "Best you go home and scrub clothes like the other women."

He stood up and glared at me. He was just three inches past five feet tall and only four months my elder. But his dark gaze was the same one I saw later on battlefields. That

8

look and those words stung—more so for their coming from a friend.

Blue and Gray got serious in July near the Virginia railroad junction of Manassas. Called it the battle of Bull Run, though to hear the men returning for furlough it wasn't much of a fight. First the Federal army broke the Southern line and hurled the graycoats back. Then this fool of a Virginian named Jackson refused to budge. Stonewall, they named him that day, and we were to hear from him again. Anyway, fresh Confederates set the Blue to running, and the next thing you knew, the whole Federal army was hightailing it toward Washington!

Was the first Sunday in August Mr. Perkins stopped by the forge after church.

"Had a letter from Enos," he told me. "Worried him some the harsh words he had with you the day before he left."

"I didn't put much stock in 'em," I said, warming to know it bothered Enos, too. "I'd tell him so if you think a letter might reach him."

"Isn't possible where he is now," Mr. Perkins explained. "A Yankee cannonball took off his head at Manassas. My brother Gabriel's buried him in Virginia. I'm taking my Emily and the little ones down to pay our respects."

"That's double hard news," I said, sighing as I remembered Pat.

"It would have been a comfort to him, recalling your friendship, Ransom. Now it's best I get along."

"Maybe I could stop at the farm later, help with harvest."

"I sold the farm, son. Too many memories for Emily. And too many Yanks for my taste."

I tried to nod, but I couldn't manage it. Later, when I told Ollie and his pa, we said a prayer for Enos.

Ever afterward the war news struck close. I had nightmares of Enos looking for his head. I dreamed of lines of bayonets headed for Frostburg. But the new year brought great Northern victories. New Orleans was taken. In April General U.S. Grant recovered from a reb attack on the Tennessee River and whipped old Beauregard's rebs south. In the east, Richmond was in danger.

Only in the Shenandoah Valley did Southern arms prevail. That same Stonewall Jackson who'd stopped the Federal army at Bull Run outwitted three Union armies in turn and roamed the valley at will. It wasn't that far from Winchester, Virginia, to Maryland, and people were talking of the threat wherever you went.

"I have a sad announcement," Mr. Havers seemingly said daily as he told of this boy or that who'd been struck down. Wasn't a month went by without somebody's brother or uncle or pa dying. This time was different, though. I could tell.

"Who is it this time, Mr. Havers?" Ollie asked.

"No one's died, thank the Lord," our teacher said. "But as the fortunes of war ebb, I can no longer remain quietly behind. I've accepted a commission from the Fourth Maryland, United States forces. Mrs. Constance Caverly will be assuming my duties here."

"No!" I cried.

"Ransom Powell, I expect you to be of great help to Mrs. Caverly," he scolded me. "You and the older students will have to help her get acquainted with our school. She hasn't had occasion to teach before."

It was a nightmare come to life. Mr. Havers was leaving us in the hands of the half-deaf mother of the postmaster.

"They got room in the Fourth for a drummer?" Ollie

10

asked when he and I stood with Mr. Havers after school let out. "I'm musical, Pa says, and I practiced some with the town band."

Truth was, it was *me* beat the drum in that band, and Ollie could scarce carry a tune in the church choir.

"No drummers needed," Mr. Havers told us. "But I'm allowed an orderly and a clerk. Actually, boys, I thought of you. Speak with your fathers and let me know. I depart day after tomorrow, so don't be long letting me know."

I stared at Ollie. He gazed at me. Orderly? Clerk? What sort of soldier was that!

"I know what you're thinking," Mr. Havers said, frowning. "You're both just thirteen, though. Prove yourselves and get some size. There's time for an officer's commission later."

Ollie brightened, and he raced off to tell his pa. I trudged along homeward wondering which was worse—helping Widow Caverly school little ones or writing letters for Lieutenant Havers.

Pa and Ma made the decision.

"I know a boy of thirteen's in a hurry to grow up," Ma told me, "but Ransom, son, you're hardly four feet tall. Just a child."

"You don't know what this war will be," Pa added. "You've never known such rough living, such coarse food and bitter cold."

"Mr. Havers'd look after me," I argued.

"He would so long as he's not drilled with a musket ball," Pa grumbled.

"I know you feel left behind," Ma said, "what with Enos first and now Ollie likely to go, but it's a fine thing staying behind if that means being alive."

11

"Can't be forever staying behind," I argued. "It's not my fault I'm small. I can still fight."

"This war's a far sight from won," Pa said, sighing. "You'll have your chance, only wait for some size, Ranse."

I nodded, but I sneaked out early that next morning and did my best to lie my way into the army.

"Ranse, your pa knows you too well," Mr. Havers remarked. "He visited me last evening and warned you were sure to try and enlist. We take no one under fifteen now unless their parents sign papers for them. I'm afraid you'll just have to wait."

It wasn't in me, though, especially when I saw Ollie all decked out in his fine blue wool, with a smart-looking kepi atop his head and as proud a gaze as I'd ever seen. The fact that he was eight inches taller was wasted on my impatient soul.

Was May when Captain Jayroe visited Frostburg. He brought along a wagon and was signing up farmboys and miners for a new regiment of loyal Virginians.

"Tenth Regiment, Virginia Unionists, we're to be called," he told me when I helped him water his horse outside the forge. "My company forms at Piedmont, Virginia."

"My name's Ransom J. Powell," I told him. "I've been looking to join up myself."

"You?" he asked with raised eyebrows. "How old are you?"

"Fifteen," I lied, recalling Mr. Havers's words.

"Can you beat a drum?" he asked.

I dashed into the barn and produced my sticks. In short order I tapped a tune or two on my knee.

"Not bad," he said, scowling. "But fifteen?"

"I run smallish," I argued.

"You'd be smallish at twelve, Powell. But as it happens, we'll need a boy to beat the drum. Can you cook?"

"Not much," I confessed.

"Read and write?"

"Good as anybody I know."

"Talk it over with your family then. And if they're agreeable to the notion, join us in Piedmont. You understand?"

"Yes, sir," I assured him.

I didn't talk over anything with Pa. Nor Ma, either, knowing their views. I wrote them a letter with my goodbyes in it, and I tucked it under Ma's teakettle in the kitchen. Then, with dark draped over Frostburg, I kissed little Jamie goodnight and slipped out of the bed we shared.

"Ranse?" he whispered.

"Go back to sleep," I urged. "Just got a call to make on the chamber pot."

"Yeah?" he said, giggling.

I did just that, then waited for him to doze off. I slipped into my best trousers, buttoned up a good cotton shirt, dumped my spare woolen drawers in a flour sack together with two books and some writing paper, and escaped out the back door. It was twenty miles to Piedmont. I'd have to walk all night to get there in time.

2

I arrived in Piedmont on the Maryland-Virginia border red-eyed and footsore. There was only a hint of light on the eastern horizon, so I found a wooden porch in front of a small general mercantile store and stretched out beneath the place's big front window.

I might have slept right through a thunderstorm. I was that tired. However, a bewhiskered shopkeeper nudged me awake with the toe of his boot.

"Hey, you, git!" he hollered with a scowl. "I look like an innkeeper? It's eight o'clock. I got customers comin', and ain't a one of 'em wants to step over you to get inside!"

"Sorry," I said, scrambling to my feet. "Know where the Tenth is mustering?"

"You ain't goin' to join them Yankees, is you, boy?" the merchant cried. "Don't you know ole Stonewall's sure to gobble up any green regiment and spit it out chewed? And you never knowin' the touch of a razor on yer chin."

"Doesn't look to me like you've known one either," I responded.

"Sassy for a Yank," he muttered. "Head on down to the church and turn left. They got a camp down that way for such riffraff as'll take to the wrong side. Best hurry 'cause Stonewall's sure to run you all past Pittsburgh 'fore summer's out."

Weren't all the Piedmont folk so friendly. Down at the church a fair portion of the women hooted and jeered a blue-coat corporal and a party of men fetching water from a well.

"Get yerselves north to Boston wid de rest o' dem abolitionists!" one old crone hollered.

I fell in with the boys, and one of the younger soldiers gave me a shove.

"Get along, little reb," he growled. "Had enough o' you."

"I'm no reb," I told them as I dusted myself off. "I come to sign the muster book. Captain Jayroe enlisted me in Frostburg."

"Lord, ain't there anybody with size fer him to bring us out o' Maryland?" the corporal cried.

"Give me a try before you send me packing," I replied. "You don't any of you appear to be so much."

"He's right, you know," the corporal mumbled. "Miserable batch of soldiers we make, eh, boys?"

They then set down their buckets and fell upon me as a group. I was fair pummeled before I managed to kick one in the shin, bite a second one's elbow, and scurry away to the far side of the road.

"Go home, youngster," the corporal urged. "Ain't war come to Maryland yet. No reb ever stole yer horses nor burned yer barn."

"Leave him be," a freckle-faced private said. "He stood his ground. Better'n some o' his elders did at Bull Run, I'd wager."

15

I grinned at the private, dusted myself off, and fell in with them again. Wasn't five minutes later we were at the camp. I stiffened my backbone and tried to stretch myself taller. Then I marched up to a long wooden table, gave Captain Jayroe a salute, and announced myself.

"Ransom J. Powell, here to enlist," I barked.

"Lord, Powell, you look to've fought your way here," the captain said, laughing. "He's the drummer, Sergeant Maggs. Sign him in and get him outfitted. We've less than a week left to join the regiment. Pair him with the Hays lad. They can drum each other quiet maybe."

"Yes, sir," Maggs, a giant of a grizzled sergeant, said with a sharp salute. "Sign on the line there, boy. What do they call you anyhow. Ranny?"

"Not for a while," I muttered. "Ranse sometimes. Think I'll try R. J. now I'm a soldier."

"Not a soldier yet," Maggs said as he scratched a line through the word *private* scrawled after my name. He wrote *musician* instead. "Armies need drummers, boy, but ain't a drummer yet thought himself the equal of a man with a musket. We got one drummer, and he's more trouble'n a brigade o' rebs. Best you meet him. He'll help you find some duds."

"Yes, sir," I said, saluting proudly.

"Children," Maggs growled. "Ought to pay me for mid-wifin'."

I followed the sergeant past four wagons to the camp. There were little groups of tall white tents. Nearby, long, grim-looking muskets were stacked in fours. Ten yards away, beside a large cauldron, sat a boy only a shade older than myself, though more Ollie's size.

"Meet Danny Hays," Sergeant Maggs said, nudging me

16

toward the other boy. "Hays, get Powell here outfitted. You two get busy with the captain's drums. Come tomorrow I want to hear the calls lively. Hear?"

"I hear," the boy said, rising slowly. "Powell, eh?"

"R. J. to my friends," I told him.

"Got any?" he replied. "Come on. Best we get you out o' them clothes 'fore somebody mistakes you for a reb and ventilates yer hide."

We made our way to the far side of the camp. A skinny fellow dressed in brown trousers and a collared shirt took charge of me there.

"I had a deuce of a time fitting you, Hays," the fellow complained. "Don't they sign up any normal-sized soldiers? I won't have anything that'll come close to fitting."

"Just find some suspenders then, and a pair of britches that won't be too far from the mark. You got a jacket, I know. Tried to sell it to that lady at the hotel for her little boy."

"You watch your tongue, Danny, or I'll cut it out."

"You quartermasters'd steal us sideways if nobody watched," Danny declared. "Don't forget the leggings. And boots. He's near worn his shoes through."

With Danny's help I managed to get a full issue of clothing, including a rubber blanket, two wool ones, overcoat, jacket, shirt and trousers, and a woolen forage cap with a brass bugle on the front.

"Only musicians get them," Danny declared as he took a pair of shears to my overlong trouser legs. "You really fifteen, Powell? Ain't got a chin hair to your name, and I got a cousin back home who's ten, and he's bigger'n you stretched."

"Most of fifteen," I said, grinning.

"Just fourteen myself," he whispered. "Don't dare tell 'em. They'd ship me home by first express. I prank 'em considerable. And best 'em at cards. Fair money to be made in this camp gamblin', you know. These farmers got no card sense at all."

"I don't play cards," I told him. "Ma don't hold with it."

"She ain't here," Danny said, laughing. "Now roll up them sleeves and let's have a look. Not too bad."

"Don't fit worth a copper," I announced. "And I'll never manage these drawers," I added, holding up a union suit big enough to pass for a tent.

"Pack 'em away to use for patches," Danny advised. "I got none better, and they plain rub me raw in the tender regions. You got good ones from home. Shame you got no regular belt," he added, passing me the one the quartermaster issued. It was just board blacked with polish to imitate leather. Worse, my boots were close to the same.

"We'll pick you up some good ones first chance," Danny promised. "I got an eye for spottin' trade opportunities."

And so, outfitted in clothes half again too big and looking all the world like somebody'd left me out in the rain to shrink, Danny Hays led me through camp for the others to laugh at.

"He a drummer, Cap?" the corporal I'd met earlier howled. "Can't even find his fingers in all that extra sleeve. How's he to beat at anything?"

"He'll need help washin' himself," another added.

"Well, boys, I figured Hays to be enough drummer for you scarecrows," the captain answered. "Got Powell here as a sort of mascot. Now he does make a dandy to look at, doesn't he?"

"Looks real mean, Cap," the corporal agreed.

I glared at them, and Danny whispered, "Best fix 'em early or it'll turn worse."

At noon I was assigned a mess, meaning I now ate with five other soldiers. To my horror I found they were the very soldiers who'd had the water detail that morning. The snarling corporal, John Poland, introduced me to Samuel Brooks, James Dyer, Billy Stagg, and the freckle-faced W. H. Armhult, known as Red. Wasn't a one of them so old as to be shaving regular, but they lorded their advanced years over me considerably.

"Don't take 'em to heart," Red warned when the corporal assigned me to tend the cook pot. "It passes."

I aimed to hurry it along. After Red dropped carrots and potatoes in our kettle, I dug out a pepper mill. In a short time I managed to grind enough spice to set a fair-sized state on fire.

"What you got there?" Red asked as I dropped a handful of pepper into the kettle.

"Something for the stew," I told him. "Captain said it'd ward off a fever."

"He did, did he?" Red asked suspiciously. "Wasn't Danny Hays said that?"

"No, sir. It's a sort of herb, I take it. Medicine."

I could tell he wasn't convinced. He gave the stew a wide berth. The others, though, helped themselves.

"Looks to be a hair more body to the stew today," Corporal Poland observed. "You make it, Powell?"

"Only cut up the carrots," Red explained. "Must be the herbs Cap sent over."

I near turned purple, but the soldiers merely nodded

toward the captain's camp and began gobbling. The pepper didn't hit right away. No, it waited maybe a minute or two. Then those fellows coughed and sputtered.

"Water!" the corporal screamed, clutching his throat.

They grabbed for their canteens and tried to put out the fire. Gagging and sputtering, with eyes close to popping out of their sockets, they eyed me savagely.

"Now see there," I told them. "You old fellows seem to be having some trouble digesting."

"I knew it!" Red said. "You put somethin' in the stew!"

"Poisoned!" Brooks shouted. "Boy's a reb spy!"

"Was only pepper!" I exclaimed as they attacked. "Just pepper."

The rest of the camp had a good hoot at their expense, and I found myself turned over Poland's knee and battered considerable on the backside.

The blows stung at first, but Poland lost his enthusiasm when I wouldn't cry.

"What the devil!" Poland grumbled. "Little bugger's hard as leather. My hand's gone sore."

"Give me a try," Dyer urged. "I'll bring out a tear."

"I won't cry," I said, kicking my way loose.

"Leave him be," Poland ordered when Dyer grabbed my arm. "Can't you tell? He's a soldier."

"Not by half," Dyer argued.

"Just by half," Stagg said, stepping between Dyer and me. "Size-wise. So far's heart, I'd guess him the tallest one here. Eh, Corporal?"

"I'd judge it so," Poland agreed, giving me a shake with his rough hand. "Should've noticed you leavin' that stew be. Ain't natural a boy not eatin'. Hungry?"

"Starved," I confessed.

"Have a chew on this bread," Red said, offering me the lion's share of a loaf intended for all. The others nodded, and I started in on the bread while they picked out bits of pepper from the stew and ate what they could. Tears welled up in their eyes from time to time, but they only laughed and said it was the first thing they could recall tasting in days.

"You've done some good, Powell," Sergeant Maggs told me that night when he showed me how to spread my rubber blanket beneath my bed. "Laughter's hard to come by on a campaign, and a well-done prank's better'n ten victories for soldiers."

Captain Jayroe warned me against bothering the food.

"That's the difference between sergeants and officers," Danny observed when we began our drum practice the next morning. "You heed what Sergeant Maggs tells you. You obey the cap, but don't take his words to heart. Ain't no real truth to what officers do. They strut and holler, sure, but it's all show. You'll see."

3

By the time we joined the rest of the regiment on May 24, I was pretty much schooled in the duties of a company drummer. Back in Piedmont we'd camped on our own. Now, with the rest of the Tenth Virginia Volunteers camped around us, we took on prideful airs. We were Captain Jayroe's boys, Company I, and when we polished our brass or performed drill under the watchful eyes of Colonel Harris, we aimed to do the cap proud.

There weren't many idle moments for a drummer, I learned. He was generally the first one up in the morning, for it was his duty to beat reveille. That was an easy drum call, as it happened, for the generals or whoever decided such things figured a half-asleep drummer ought not to be tempted to err. It was quite a sight when Danny and I, together with the buglers, roused the men. They stepped out in their drawers, or union suits, yawning and cursing. In minutes everyone straggled into line, mostly uniformed, while First Sergeant Cyrill Maggs called the roll.

Each man answered "here" in his most solemn and resounding voice. Then, when Danny and I took our turns, we fought not to squeak like startled mice. Danny could almost give off a man's sound when it wasn't too cold, but I still had too much boy in my voice. Even the captain smiled now and then when he heard my answers.

Following thirty minutes of drill, Danny and I beat the breakfast call. This was one of our more welcome drum rolls, but it meant we were always last to eat. My mess used to empty the pot before I got there and then make me hunt down my food. A plate was generally stowed away in the least likely spot. They got their due when the captain stopped by one morning and sat right in it, hidden as it was beneath a folded blanket.

"Sorry, Powell," Captain Jayroe told me. "I've spoiled your beans."

"And they've spoiled your pants, sir," I noted.

"As to the latter, Corporal Poland's certain to make good on all damages," he told me. "As to the former, perhaps you'll be my guest. I believe Henry's got some fresh eggs and a slab of bacon set by."

Oh, did my mess ever turn purple! Henry, the captain's cook come along from home, served up breakfast the way Ma used to when we had Sunday company. I believe I near fit my britches that morning.

All together we had ten calls to beat every day, with a few extra set aside for battles. Following breakfast there was sick call, when Maggs lined up the ailing for a march to the regimental surgeon. That also spelled time to finish with fatigue duty—policing camp and tidying quarters. All that had to be done by eight each morning because Danny and I then sounded the call for guard mount.

The rest of each morning was devoted to more drill. Yep,

23

we had a drum call to announce that, too. While the men worked the manual of arms and marched to and fro, Danny and I beat the ordered tempo or called for advance and retreat.

The day's sixth call was to dinner, but everybody took to calling it *roast beef.* "Beat us up the beef," Sergeant Maggs would cry. Danny and I would send everybody to noon mess.

In the afternoon we had still more drill and spent time brushing uniforms, blackening our "leather" belts and boots, and polishing brass. If we were to stay in one place a few days, we'd scare up leaves or pine nettles to soften the ground. If a tent had a rip, some fellow would haul out a needle and stitch her up. By then Danny and I had our own tent, made by matching his shelter half with mine, set up alongside Captain Jayroe.

Since I wrote a fair hand, sometimes I'd help the captain with his papers while Danny tended to such errands as required longer legs and less brains. On a few occasions we'd escape long enough to wash out some socks or set off on a lark.

"You're almost good company," Danny declared the day we liberated a bushel of apples from some rebel sympathizers. "And near as good at thievin' as a reb!"

That was high praise, considering the rebel bushwhackers lived off what they could scare the farmers into offering, steal off folks loyal to our flag, or raid from us.

Retreat was the seventh call, and my favorite. That was when all the companies paraded in full dress, with arms shouldered, for Colonel Harris and his staff to inspect. Danny and I would tramp along, drumsticks whirling away, while the buglers played, and the flag bearers brought the colors out. The officers stepped out front, sabers drawn,

24

making a flashy show for visitors and convincing them and ourselves we were really an army.

When the colonel had a good look, he'd often say a few words. Occasionally some general would happen by and read us some dispatches about our glorious service at the end of retreat. Other times we'd receive news of the war, be lectured to take better care of our feet, or be warned not to steal any more chickens from the Cheat Mountain farms, as reb bushwhackers were favoring the roads there.

"Waste of time, such speechifyin'," Danny usually complained. "Too many 'high pockets' generals around, likin' to hear their own talk and keepin' us from our work."

After retreat we sounded supper call. Then later there was tattoo—another roll call, one of the army's measures to hinder twilight desertions. Taps was our final call, and its solemn beat was used at burying time, too.

"Well, why not?" Danny told me once. "Means lanterns out, noises cease, and all enlisted men in their tents. Sort of the day dyin', don't you think, R. J.?"

He had a point.

You kept busy in camp, especially if you were a drummer, but it wasn't to polish brass or move muskets off and on shoulders that any of us had joined up. It was to fight, and we all welcomed the morning when Captain Jayroe announced we were marching out to have a look for some reb bushwhackers operating near Cheat Mountain.

I, being unfamiliar with Virginia, asked Danny just where Cheat Mountain was.

"All over," he answered. "Spreads out for miles and miles." It appeared that in western Virginia they named whole ridges mountains. And as to hunting up rebs, well, it was about like picking a flea off a mangy hound. If you

25

found one, there were generally more close by. Worse, by day they'd be tending fields like a hundred other farmers. Then, once the sun fell, they'd saddle a horse and ride off to have a try at burning some depot or bridge. More and more they were after the bridges, tracks, and trestles of the Baltimore and Ohio Railroad. The B & O just so happened to be our supply tether, and we took a particular dislike to having our flour and coffee captured or burned.

It got worse when we moved up into the mountain country near Beverly in July. Seemed like every shadow or rock hid a reb, and we dared not set off alone after dark. Two privates from Company B got themselves captured while visiting nature, and thereafter we posted guards everywhere—even around the sinks.

Mostly we marched to some farm or house where a reb leader was suspected of living. We arrested one or two those first few days, mostly from information passed to us by loyal citizens. Thereafter the rebs caught on. One day while storming a house that was supposed to harbor a band of rebs, we found ourselves surrounding the district superintendent of the B & O. We took a harder look at informants after that.

The first trouble Company I had with any bushwhackers was along toward September. We were camped near Bulltown, and what with news General Robert E. Lee's army was loose in Maryland, I was itching to fight.

"They could be burning my house right now," I complained.

"Oh, they're off toward Frederick," Sergeant Maggs told me by way of comfort. "I'd guess 'em bound for Washington, or even Baltimore. And there's plenty of army up that way eager to tend things."

But I was tired of marching around in the wilds, hunting an enemy that never fought in the open. Stonewall Jackson's romp through the Shenandoah Valley and Lee's invasion of Maryland had emboldened the bushwhackers, though. And the same day we heard of Lee's defeat at Antietam Creek in Maryland, we found ourselves beset by thirty or forty riders while off cutting wood.

"Sound your drum good and loud, Powell!" Sergeant Maggs ordered. "We could do with some help."

Corporal Poland, meanwhile, rallied what handful of men hadn't run off and left their muskets. I kept to Maggs's shadow, beating my drum as he gave commands. Pretty soon the rebs charged, but all they got for their trouble was a hot spray of lead.

"Grab those guns and let's go!" the reb captain yelled as he waved his plumed hat at us. It was about the only shred of uniform any of them owned. Then, after a final exchange of fire, the bushwhackers rode off into the brush, leaving us to recover our wits.

"Who's hurt?" Sergeant Maggs barked, and two men hobbled over. They'd each caught a ball through a leg, and we loaded them onto a pair of captured horses and took them back to camp. One poor fellow name of Hopkinson had worse luck. He was shot right through the head— killed outright.

"Our first man lost to enemy fire," Captain Jayroe announced while Danny and I beat taps at the burying. "His loss will not be forgotten."

But soon enough, with winter creeping into the high country and the rebs growing bolder, we had other worries.

First on my mind was the sorry state of my equipment. All the boot blacking in creation couldn't preserve the pitiful excuse for a belt I'd been issued, and by the middle of October my boots just downright disintegrated. Stockings gave up shortly thereafter, and I had to wrap my feet in blanket strips to keep from freezing.

The rest of my uniform wasn't much better. The elbows of my tunic were worn through, and if the seat of my trousers got any thinner, I'd be pure embarrassed. The only piece of clothing that was still whole was the woolen drawers I brought from Frostburg.

The rest of the men were as bad off—or worse. It got cold in the mountains, and the line at sick call grew longer. Captain Jayroe did his best to arrange furloughs so one batch or another could go home and get outfitted proper for winter.

"We've got some wagons headed for Cumberland," he told me one evening as Danny and I prepared to crawl into our blankets. "Care for a trip home, Powell?"

"Wouldn't likely be free to come back," I told him. "I didn't exactly have their blessing when I left."

"Still, they'd welcome a visit, I'd wager."

"Can't go losin' a proper trained drummer, Cap," Danny argued. "You know he ain't of age. His ma'd likely dish out a spankin' and get some senator to manage his discharge."

"It could happen," I added.

"Well, we have to do something about you two," the captain grumbled. "We've had complaints from the ladies of Beverly that you two show a hair more flesh than's proper. They can't keep their daughters at chores. Too busy dreaming of young bluecoats."

"Can't be dreaming about me," I insisted. "I'm but a mere child, after all."

"Oh?" Captain Jayroe cried. "It's you they squawk about

28

most of all, Powell. Those amber curls and big blue eyes just naturally set a female's heart to fluttering. Now don't let me hear you've offered them any encouragement."

"Who's got the time?" I asked, grinning.

"Oh, they all look like sows anyway," Danny muttered.

"Not all," the cap said with a wink. "I'll speak to the quartermasters about some new britches at least."

"Boots, Captain," I told him. "My toes freeze most every day."

"I know, son. But finding a pair of boots of any size requires divine intervention, and matching your feet, Powell, well, we'll all of us have to pray a good deal harder and do a lot less sinning."

As it happened, my clothing problem got solved the very next day. Corporal Poland, Red, Sam Brooks, and I were making the rounds of Beverly when a girl shouted at us. She was dressed in calico and looked to be a relative of Danny's, what with her strawberry freckles and light hair.

"Go see what she wants, R. J.," Red suggested, and I slung my drum over my shoulder and hurried to the rail fence that lined her property.

"Li'l Yank, you look threadbare," she told me with a smile.

"I've seen better days," I confessed. "But we've marched down here to put an end to the rebellion, and I don't suppose you need Sunday suits for that."

"Doesn't mean you have to go naked," she said, reaching out and tapping my bare right elbow. "For myself, I wish you all'd go home and leave us be. But it says in the Book 'thou shalt clothe the stranger,' so I expect that applies to Yanks as much as anybody else."

I scratched my head. Never once did I recall hearing that

verse. Anyway, she latched hold of my arm and drug me to her house. Next thing I knew, she'd gotten me in a closet, with brooms and mops and such, and ordered me to shed my rags.

"I will not," I told her. Then I howled for help. That brazen mountain gal only laughed and started working my buttons.

"All right!" I exclaimed. "You win. Get yourself back the other side of this door, and I'll hand 'em out."

"I seen boys before, you know," she told me. "Got five brothers."

"I'm not one of them," I said, "and if you stick your head back here, I'll make Antietam Creek look like a skirmish!"

Later I felt almost bad for saying that, as she really did have my welfare at heart. I'd never been able to abide a bossy girl, though, especially when she put on airs and went to barking orders like a major general!

In the end, I wound up with a good flannel shirt, and she patched my blue trousers and tunic so they looked almost new. Best of all she found me a pair of boots only lightly worn.

"They're my brother Jubal's things," she explained as I laced my boots. "You look like him. He's no longer in need of them."

"Outgrown?" I asked.

"No, gone off," she said, wiping her forehead.

"Where's he gone?" I asked like a fool.

"East, with the Stonewall Brigade," she said, looking through a window. "Killed last summer. He'd be sixteen February coming."

"I lost a friend myself in the spring," I said, recalling Enos with a heavy heart. "Not the same as a brother, I

30

know, but close to. Never expected such to happen. Cannonball took off his head. He was riding with Jeb Stuart, wearing the gray."

"Was he?" she asked, brightening. "And you beatin' a Yankee drum. 'Course I'm sewin' Yankee trousers myself. This fool war's got some strange turns, don't it?"

"Yes, ma'am," I said, laughing at the notion.

"Now don't you feel silly callin' me ma'am? I'm Laurel Lee."

"People call me R. J.," I told her.

She reached over and gave me a kiss, right in the middle of my forehead. I turned purple and fell over myself scurrying away. I grabbed my drum and scampered out of her house, stumbling over my laces along the way.

"R. J.?" Laurel Lee called from the door.

"Boy, why's your face gone all red?" Poland asked as I got back on my feet.

"R. J., don't be in such a hurry," Sam added. "That gal there'd be happy to help you lace them boots. Might help you get your drawers on, even."

They had a fine hoot at my expense, but in the end I had my mended duds and new boots, didn't I?

I saw Laurel Lee twice more before Christmas. Once she offered me some cotton stockings as we marched along the road. I passed her by, but Danny rushed over and fetched them. Later on she sent me a better pair of trousers with Sergeant Maggs, and he insisted I pay her a visit and offer my thanks.

"Closest call I had since those reb bushwhackers took after us," I told Danny afterward. "I believe she intended to recruit me for General Bob Lee. And failing that, to choke me."

"Just how'd she go about that?" Danny asked.

"That's one secret nobody'll pry out of me."

He laughed considerably, and by nightfall I was famous throughout the regiment.

Off and on since leaving home I'd suffered a shudder or two of the lonelies. Now, with Christmas coming and the first snow flurries of winter haunting the mountains, I began to get downright homesick.

"Cap'd give you a furlough," Danny told me one night when my thrashing around in my blankets woke him. "Maybe you ought to go home for a time."

"Wouldn't likely be coming back," I mumbled.

"Then you sit down and write a letter. Lord, R. J., I wish to high heaven I had somebody carin' whether I came home or wrote. Write 'em."

Captain Jayroe said pretty much the same thing next morning.

"Somebody put time in on you, son. You've had education and manners. Tell them why you signed on. I've got a feeling they'll understand, although I don't know what madness sends a boy out to freeze himself in these godforsaken mountains. If nothing else, tell them nobody's put a bullet in your hide yet.

"I'm going to share some truth with you, Powell. That devil Lee just slaughtered ten thousand of our men at Fredericksburg. To hear tell, the long lines of blue kept coming up those hills in perfect order for the rebs to cut down. *Courage. Glory.* Those words hold a hollow tone when you stare at a mountainside of dead friends."

"It'll be hard, the writing," I told him.

"I've had to write a few letters that were a whole lot harder," he said, resting a hand on my shoulder. "Better

32

they should get a friendly one from you first, don't you suppose?"

"Think the rebs'll get me, Cap?"

"Some mighty sharp shots among those bushwhackers, Powell. They can even hit small targets. And we may not be in these hills forever. Word has it General Burnside needs soldiers to make up the losses at Fredericksburg. We could be headed east ourselves."

"Ten thousand, Cap?" I asked. We'd all heard news of the Fredericksburg defeat, but nobody'd mentioned numbers. I'd never in my life been in a town with that many people. I couldn't imagine such a number in the first place, much less dead.

"Tell them I said you've been an example to the men," he whispered. "And that you serve your country proudly. Isn't true," he added, laughing. "But tell them I said it."

I looked up at him and grinned. And seeing the far-off gaze in his eyes, I knew thirteen-year-olds weren't the only ones got a touch of the lonelies on a long campaign.

The captain was mighty generous with furloughs that Christmas of '62, but I stayed just the same. Danny wouldn't have had anyone to get him into trouble if I'd gone, and the two of us did a fair job of keeping the company entertained, drumming out marches and singing hymns. We favored the captain every night, for he was missing his family. And twice Colonel Harris stopped by for our concert.

"Nothing warms like a fine song, son," the colonel told me as he placed a silver dollar in my hand. "God bless you, boy."

"Powell, you break an ole sinner's heart," Corporal Poland said when Danny and I sang for the men New Year's Eve. "Got me to missin' my brothers."

He sat in my tent later on, telling me all about his farm and family. I was suspicious of a prank at first, for that man had provided more than a few vexations. Then I saw he was actually crying.

"Bet they miss you, too," I finally said.

"Will especially come plantin' time," Poland said. "Hard life, farmin' these cussed hills. But a man knows where he is, workin' the land."

He was still talking when Danny brought me a cup of hot cider. I offered Poland a sip, but he judged my need greater.

"You put us all to shame, Powell. Skinny boy like you standin' up to everything we throw yer way. I swear you'll suffer no longer at the hands of Corporal John Poland."

He meant it, too. An hour short of daybreak Poland took French leave of the company. He wasn't the only one to desert that winter, but the captain took it ill losing a corporal, a man he'd trusted.

"Just went home to plant his fields," I told Danny.

"In January?" Danny cried. "Long time till plantin'."

"Maybe he wanted to be sure he was still in one piece in April," I said, frowning.

"Figure anybody will be?" Danny asked. "I hear we've got marchin' orders."

"I was tired of these good, soft pine needles anyway," I muttered. "Night or two on the cold hard ground's sure to be welcome."

Danny threw his hat at me.

4

We passed the first four months of 1863 in Winchester, Virginia, guarding the B & O, skirmishing with graycoat cavalry, and chasing bushwhackers out of their hilly nests. We were part of General Milroy's brigade at first, paired up with other loyal Virginia regiments to make a small army. Our guarding the north stretch of the Shenandoah Valley comforted the politicians in Washington and gave heart to the Unionists in Virginia and Maryland.

I had a half dozen letters from home while we were in Winchester, and Ma sent a good wool shirt, some heavy boot socks, and a flannel nightshirt. My sisters baked a cake for my birthday that they smuggled aboard a quartermaster wagon and got to me somehow. The food and clothing were welcome, but it was the words that most cheered me.

"Your pa boasts most pridefully of his son, the soldier," Ma wrote. "And you've certainly become the darling of my sewing circle. We'll soon send you knitted stockings and trousers that will fit, and Mary's gone with Agnes Fair to Cumberland in search of boots."

She spoke of prayers and hopes. And urged me against being foolish.

"Ollie came back at Christmas to tell of how our brave Mr. Havers charged the rebels at Antietam, only to be struck down most horribly."

Ollie himself had two toes shot off his left foot.

"We've had better luck ourselves," I wrote back. "Only three men dead, and two of them by sickness. Our biggest enemies are the food and the insects."

In March I got acquainted with sick call. Like I said, the food was on the weak side, and I came down with what the army called the valley one-step. In our regiment, it was known as the Tenth trots. Diarrhea! Lord, got so you hardly chewed a biscuit but that part of it was on its way out of you. Your stomach knotted up, bending you double. And you stayed that way till you just paled to nothing.

Sergeant Maggs threw me over a shoulder and carried me off to the hospital. Was a third of the regiment down with the trots, and the surgeons were at the end of their tether.

"Powell, you look bad," Captain Jayroe observed when he paid me a call.

"Sorry I missed retreat," I told him.

"Never you worry over that. Men twice as big are dying here. Just wasting away to nothing. I think it best we furlough you home. You'd be welcome, I suspect."

"Might not be allowed to come back," I pointed out.

"Maybe that would be best," he replied. "We're headed into some serious business soon, and it's sure to whittle on our numbers. Be a considerable test for a boy your size."

"You don't think I'm fit for it?" I asked, frowning.

"Game as a fighting cock, Powell, but none too sturdy. It would trouble me to lose you."

36

"I'm not easy to lose," I countered. "And I'll get well. Maybe next Christmas I'll take your furlough—if the war's not finished."

Danny managed to buy me some kind of root off an old hill woman, and he brewed it up into a tea. It dried me out in a single day, and I was beating my drum again by week's end.

"Thanks," I told my tentmate.

"You'd do the same for me," he said, grinning. "Besides, it's too cold not havin' anybody in the blankets next to me. I tried beddin' down by Red and Sam, but they snore awful."

"You snore yourself, Danny."

"Not so I'd wake the dead."

The cold was another vexation. Winter was wicked in Winchester, and even once we were quartered in a stable, the icy touch of the north wind found our ribs.

"Consider yourselves lucky," Sergeant Maggs told me when Danny and I complained. "Cavalry patrol yesterday found four rebs frozen stiff down past the valley pike. Not shot. Just froze."

It was poor comfort, knowing the rebs had it worse. I was every inch as cold as the night before.

In May the new commander of the Army of the Potomac, General Hooker, slipped around the rebs entrenched at Fredericksburg and started after Richmond. Fighting Joe, as they called him, had a hundred and twenty thousand men, as I heard it, and Bob Lee was hard-pressed to muster half that many. It looked like the rebs in the east would finally meet with Union justice, but that Lee was a fox. Out past a place called Chancellorsville, in a tangle of briers called the Wilderness, Stonewall Jackson came charging out of nowhere and threw the whole Potomac army into a rout. Next thing we knew Hooker was reeling backward, and the rebs were on the march north. Only good thing to happen was ole Jackson got himself shot—by his own men, it was said. You knew he had died from the black drapes hanging outside the reb houses in Winchester.

It was about that time the Tenth got itself transferred to General Averell. Officially we were now part of the Second Division, Eighth Army Corps. They gave us a six-pointed white star to sew on our sleeves to mark the occasion. And Averell sent us back to Beverly to campaign against the bushwhackers some more.

Averell was a cavalryman, and three of the brigade's regiments got themselves mounted. We stayed afoot, which was just fine by me. Growing up a smith's son, I'd seen plenty of horses, and there wasn't a one of them I trusted. You shot bullets around animals, and they got downright troublesome. Never saw so many broken-legged soldiers as when the Second Virginia Cavalry got their mounts.

"At least it'd liven up camp life," Danny grumbled. "All we do's drill and march and wait."

That changed, though. By summer the Shenandoah Valley was in an uproar. Old General Milroy got half his command captured at Winchester by the vanguard of Lee's army on June 14. Four hundred killed and wounded. Four thousand taken prisoner, a fifth of them sick in hospital. Twenty-three cannons and the whole wagon train, too! It was like Stonewall had risen from the dead. He'd grabbed the Harper's Ferry garrison the summer before just that same way!

Meanwhile, General Averell was having a try at a couple of rebel regiments opposite Beverly. He had his cavalry off chasing one group or another. The Tenth, being infantry, was split off by companies and left to guard wagons and the precious B & O tracks. Nowadays we did less drilling, though. Mainly we dug trenches or patrolled the woods in squads.

It was in June we learned the Federal Congress had decided to welcome into its body the spanking new state of West Virginia. Thereafter we were officially the Tenth West Virginia Volunteer Infantry. General Averell had his horse soldiers chasing rebs out of what were now the border counties between the new state and old Virginia, and we found ourselves getting plenty of attention from the ones that slipped past our cavalry.

More times than I could remember, Sergeant Maggs or the captain roused Danny and me from our sleep with orders to beat assembly. We scrambled to our feet, half-dressed, and sounded the calls. Then we raced back and got our uniforms on.

"Me, I don't aim to pass eternity in my underwear!" Danny remarked as he put fingers through some dollar-sized holes in his union suit.

"More holes'n cloth there, Danny," Red cried, and Danny took on the nickname "Holy Brother" ever afterward. Me, they'd dubbed "Runnin' Ranny" after my battle with the trots.

That summer was a trial in other ways, too. Lee tramped through Maryland, foraging considerably, even burning some towns, before crashing up against George Meade at Gettysburg, Pennsylvania. Pa sent Mary, Nancy, and little Jamie out to Ohio for a while.

Was after Gettysburg we got word Grant had taken Vicksburg on the Fourth of July. Those two victories promised great things, and our spirits soared. Then, on July 22, Johnny Poland came marching into our camp.

"Get the crop in, Poland?" Maggs asked.

"Sure did," the corporal said, laughing. "Figured I'd best come back and keep you boys on the mark now."

The men laughed at Poland's easy manner and the hand-stitched shirt he'd gotten off a neighbor girl. Captain Jayroe wasn't near so forgiving.

"You're a deserter, Poland," Cap grumbled when he tore the twin yellow stripes off Poland's jacket. "You'll serve company punishment. Lucky not to be shot."

"Can't fight rebs dead," Poland argued. "Anyhow, I'd have come back before but I couldn't get through all them rebs movin' past my farm. Bound for Gettysburg, I guess."

So Meade's winning at Gettysburg brought the Tenth Johnny Poland. In the valley itself, victories proved hard to come by.

It was at Sutton near the end of August that we fought a real battle of sorts. Oh, we'd driven the rebs off from New Creek and shot up our share of bushwhackers. But with Company G at our side, we crashed up against regular Virginia cavalry. Those devils rode down on us out of a fog, screaming and waving sabers around. We were all of us shook, but Captain Jayroe held his ground.

"Beat the drums, boys!" he hollered at Danny and me. "Give the men something to steady themselves."

I thumped my sticks against that drum with all the fury I could manage, and Danny did the same.

"Hope they stop 'em, R. J.," Danny told me all the while. "I ain't eager to get myself pig stuck with a reb sword."

It seemed the rebel charge broke itself against our lines. Then a wail of musketry shook us from the flank. I winced as a ball clipped my drum and stung my fingers with splinters.

40

"Run!" Danny howled as three riders bore down on us, firing away with pistols. I hadn't gotten an order to leave, though, and I stood my ground. Danny reached back, grabbed my belt, and dragged me into the cover of some trees. By and by the rebs rode off, and when the smoke cleared, we were still holding the road to Sutton.

"Is it over?" I asked when I spotted Captain Jayroe. His left sleeve was torn, and he'd lost his hat. A smile came to his lips when he spotted Danny and me, though.

"Powell, you've ripped your pants," he said, pointing to a gash above my right knee. "Rebs?"

"Briers," Danny said, hauling me to my feet.

"Go help tend the wounded now," the captain ordered. "It's a busy time's ahead."

Danny and I made our way down the line, offering water from a dipper or wrapping cloth around wounds. I expected dozens killed, and many wounded, but in the end we fared rather well. A few men got scratched up, and three were shot. Others were killed—shot or cut down by sabers. We found half a dozen rebs on the field, too. Company G reported some more out their way.

"Not many when you think of the thousands killed in the east," Captain Jayroe muttered. It chafed him we were still fighting a backwater war.

"Not so many to bury, either, Cap," Sergeant Maggs pointed out.

It seemed enough when Danny and I beat taps beside the trench where we buried our dead. We surprised some of the men by having a go at "Dixie" while the chaplain read over the dead rebs.

"Ain't the enemy no more," Danny declared. Me, I was just glad no one from my mess got killed.

Autumn sent the company to Petersburg. It was just a little supply town, and we didn't have much action there. At least not from rebs. Our camp was down by a creek, in a sort of swamp, and soon two-thirds of us were sick. This time Danny took fever before I did, but I barely started nursing him when I boiled over with it myself.

"Tertian fever," the local doctor declared when Captain Jayroe brought him out. "Get your camp to dry ground. Try sweating out the fever. And dose 'em with quinine."

"Can't you do it?" Cap asked.

"Son, I haven't seen quinine since the war started up," the doctor said, scratching his scraggly white beard. "I'm told your medical corps has a great supply of it, though. Your surgeons will know what to do."

Since the rest of the regiment was elsewhere, it took some time for Captain Jayroe to fetch the regimental surgeon. He, too, directed us to higher ground. He ordered every scrap of clothes scrubbed with harsh lye, and we were all dosed with quinine—a bitter sort of herb that passed a close second as the nastiest tonic I'd ever tasted. That tea Danny'd made back in Winchester took first easy.

Tertian fever was a time working its way through me. Strange thing, tertian fever. Burned you up with fever and then shook you half to death with cold. Then it went away for two days and hit you all over again the third.

I had a light case of it, as it turned out, but Danny near melted away before my eyes. I'd about given up on him, when Maggs brought that same old hill woman to camp, and she ordered us to take him fevered to the creek and wash him proper. Maggs and I held his head up while she worked over Danny with a horsehair brush and some tonics that smelled like sulphur.

"He ain't so big as I thought," the sergeant said, squeezing my shoulder. "Ain't right bringin' boys to war."

"Ever read the Bible?" I asked.

"Some," he confessed.

"Always been boys fighting wars. David slew Goliath when all the men were scared. Sooner or later this would've been our fight."

"Maybe," he admitted. "But later you'd've been bigger, R. J. And maybe I wouldn't have had to watch Danny here shiver his life away."

That hill woman knew her trade, however. Every soldier she doctored took a turn for the better. She wound up riding the captain's best horse back home, hauling two pack mules loaded down with whatever she asked for.

"You boys up to a hard campaign?" Captain Jayroe asked us as November loomed on the horizon.

"Can't be worse'n stayin' 'round here," Danny barked.

"Then get your fingers limbered. We break camp and rejoin the regiment. There's real fighting in the air."

"Yes, sir," I shouted, saluting. And Danny actually smiled.

If he'd known what lay ahead, Danny never would have wasted a smile. We marched back toward Beverly, retracing our steps for what seemed the hundredth time. Cap counted 420 miles we marched all total in that fall campaign. This time we marched hard and far, wearing out our shoes and leaving anything we could spare on the trail. Danny and I were luckier than most, for the captain often hauled one or the other of us up behind him on his horse.

"Quittin' the foot cavalry, R. J.?" Red Armhult, now corporal in Poland's place, called out.

"The barefoot cavalry's more like it," I answered, showing where my toes protruded through the remnants of Jubal's boots.

"We'll have equipment waiting for us at Huntersville," Captain Jayroe explained. "Truth is, I've eaten so much of you boys' cooking there's not enough of me left to keep a horse exercised. I do miss Henry."

Cap's cook had returned home when we'd left Winchester. We'd all hated to see that man go.

As it happened, we didn't have the time to reequip ourselves at Huntersville. No, General Averell was up against Colonel W. L. Jackson and the Fourteenth Virginia Cavalry. The rebs had infantry, too, all stretched across Droop Mountain.

"Those rebs and their Jacksons!" Colonel Harris exclaimed. "Well, this one's yet to prove he's of Stonewall's mettle. Shall we show them what the Tenth's made of, boys?"

We cheered and tossed our hats. But deep down I was nervous. This wasn't any skirmish or chase we were starting. It was a regular battle.

"Scared?" Danny asked the November morning when we assembled Company I in battle formation.

"A hair," I said, fighting to concentrate on my drumming.

"Smell the air," Danny urged. I did and recoiled. It was cold, and there was snow under the taller trees left from an earlier storm. The company was sweating. We were all frightened.

I could tell Cap knew it, too. He waved his hat and rode along our line, urging calm, swapping jokes, making fun of our shabby uniforms.

"It's a hard fight coming," he called as he motioned Danny and me out in front of the men. "About time. I've

44

had the devil's own time keeping these two drummers here on a leash. Powell complains he'll be old and shaving before the rebs stand up and fight us."

"We got to wait that long?" Poland called. "I'll be a swaybacked old man by then."

"Oh, them rebs'll fight once they know Powell's with us," Cap said, winking in my direction. "Got to. Otherwise their womenfolk are sure to run off, seeing the fine figure of manhood we have here beating a drum."

"That me or R. J.?" Danny called.

"Best watch those youngsters," Maggs warned. "They'll steal yer thunder, Cap."

A rider brought orders then, and silence settled over the line. The brigade was formed in a crescent, with the cavalry facing the enemy. The Twenty-eighth Ohio was moving out ahead of us on a zigzag sort of path up the side of Droop Mountain. We followed. If all went well we'd wind up to the flank and rear of the reb infantry and fall on them with a fury.

We followed the plan, all right, but that prickly country wasn't made for fighting. Our line simply dissolved, mixing itself with Company G, running into the Ohioans after a time, cluttering the hillside with bluecoats, and all the while fighting to keep quiet lest we tip our hand to the rebs.

Was around two o'clock that afternoon when the Twenty-eighth charged. They soon drove back the reb pickets. For a few minutes skirmishers fired away, and we could hear something that sounded like green logs popping on a fresh fire. Then suddenly the air filled with a terrible whine as rebs leaped out of their trenches and charged into the Ohioans.

The Twenty-eighth wasn't any more used to that sort of a

fight than we were, and the rebs pressed their advantage. Whole companies of the Twenty-eighth fought to escape the weight of rebel arms, and in the process they tangled themselves in the brush and got shot to pieces.

"Colonel Harris, bring your men forward!" an animated man wearing a plumed hat shouted as he dashed by on horseback. It was General Averell. "Work your way free of the Twenty-eighth and come around to the rebels' rear."

"Yes, sir," the colonel said, saluting. Next thing I knew Danny and I were beating the advance. Captain Jayroe pulled us around on the far side of Company A. I had to set my sticks in my belt as I clawed through the dense forest. Then we came upon a sandy road and re-formed. Already the lead companies of the Tenth were tangling with graycoats. The captain led us past torn branches and smoldering underbrush. I stepped cautiously past a line of intertwined soldiers, some wearing blue and others gray. All were dead. Then we reached a stretch of abandoned trench.

"There they are, boys!" Captain Jayroe said, pointing to a confused gray line struggling against the pressures of Companies A and B. Danny and I drummed, and confused rebs turned toward the new threat. Sergeant Maggs formed the company in three successive lines, and the men balanced their rifles as they had a hundred times before. A thunderous crash rocked the reb line. Graycoats fell back, but fresh ones took their place. Again, fire spit from rifles. We moved forward, one line after another firing and then slipping back to reload. Powder smoke stung my eyes, clawed at my throat. Still I drummed, and we moved onward.

I don't exactly know when the first of us fell. But that's what broke the company's discipline. This green young lieutenant named Ahem brandished his sword and led one batch after a handful of skulking graycoats. Then the rest of the company rushed forward.

"Form up!" Captain Jayroe ordered, slapping his horse toward the charge. "Stop and form!"

Then the rebs came out of the woods on my right.

I don't suppose there were more than two dozen, but I felt as if Bob Lee's whole army was after us. After me! There I was, with just the drum for protection. First a bullet nicked my coat. Another sliced the straps holding the drum, and it fell.

I froze. Then I turned to Danny.

"Run!" he howled.

But before he could turn, the rebs were on top of us.

"Danny!" I screamed as somebody threw me backward. I landed on my drum, and the breath rushed out of me. Danny fell on his side a foot away. His hat slid off his head, and he stared at me with those clear, thoughtful green eyes of his. Blood stained his yellow hair and trickled out the corner of his mouth.

"Ranny?" he whispered, reaching out and clasping my hand.

"Here," I managed to say as my fingers clawed his. I stared up into the face of a grizzled old-timer who was poised to crush my chest with a musket butt. There wasn't even time to pray. Then Sergeant Maggs arrived.

I never saw fighting like what followed. Maggs thrust his bayonet into the old rebel and flung him away like so much chaff at threshing time. He grinned to me as he fired off a shot and dropped a second Confederate. Those who were left turned and beheld the captain rushing to our aid with twenty men. But Maggs had come ahead—alone.

"What you waitin' for, rebs?" Maggs shouted. They lifted their muskets and uncorked a volley that swept the air from that hillside. Maggs was flung ten feet backward, hit by five or more balls. He didn't even flinch, just stood there and died like a first sergeant was supposed to.

"God help him," I prayed as I struggled to kick the reb old-timer from where he lay atop my legs. "Danny, did you see that?"

Danny managed to nod. Then I felt his fingers weaken. By the time Red Armhult and Sam Brooks got to us, I'd pulled Danny against me, hoping somehow my own strength might flow into him.

"He's left us, R. J.," Red said, prying my fingers loose. "Shot through the side and nicked in the temple."

I wouldn't listen. There was Danny, my best friend, who taught me the drum calls, who nursed me when I took sick, who . . .

"Powell, beat the recall!" Captain Jayroe commanded. "The men are scattering. Are you a soldier or a child?"

"Cap, can't you—" Red started to explain.

"Now, Powell!" the captain shouted.

I reached over and took my sticks off the ground. Danny's blood dripped off my shoulder, mixing with the tears dribbling off my chin. They mixed in swirls on the surface of the drum as I obeyed orders and sounded the recall. Meanwhile Red bent down and closed Danny's eyelids.

"They got Maggs, too," Red explained when the captain motioned for me to stop.

"I saw it," Captain Jayroe replied. "Powell, he must have thought an awful lot of you to run ahead like that and bring down the whole bunch of them on him."

"Knew he'd be killed," Sam said, lifting my chin.

48

"Danny's dead," I whimpered.

"It appears we've suffered mightily to take this mountain," Cap said, offering me his hand. "Come ride a bit, son."

"Best I stay with Danny," I replied. "If duty allows."

"It does," Red said, pulling me to his side. "Don't it, Cap?"

Captain Jayroe nodded. I believe there'd have been a fight if he'd said otherwise. The smoke began to clear, and the moans of the wounded began to torture the air.

"Sit yourself down and wring the sadness out of you," Red advised. "And come nightfall, you head over and spread your blankets with Sam and me. Ain't a night to be alone, R. J."

I nodded my silent thanks, then sat beside Danny and remembered. That was the easy part. Forgetting would be harder.

5

We buried Danny Hays and Cyrill Maggs side by side in the rocky soil of Droop Mountain, a few paces from the other six men of the Tenth who'd been killed in the attack. I beat taps sadder than I'd ever expected possible. Colonel Harris gave a moving speech, and General Averell himself paid us a visit to cheer our efforts.

After a rather sleepless night, squeezed between Red Armhult and Sam Brooks, I collected my wits and beat assembly. Soon we were marching to Lewisburg. We must have made a fearful sight, marching in columns with drums beating. Not a one of us had managed a wash, and we wore our bloodstained tunics and powder-blackened faces as a sort of testament to our courage.

We hardly caught our breath before accompanying the Twenty-eighth Ohio to Beverly. Once again the infantry was assigned to guard supplies and the rail lines. We also had charge of the brigade's wounded and about a hundred reb prisoners. When I wasn't beating the calls, Captain Jayroe had me helping Surgeon Blair tend the wounded. I also passed some time taking water to the reb captives.

Most of those pitiful scarecrows weren't much older than I was. They looked up at me, nodded their thanks for the water, and stared in a far-off sort of way.

"Thanks, Yank," one would say.

Another might offer a plug of tobacco.

"Got cousins in Maryland," a shaggy-haired fellow explained when I told them I was from Frostburg. "Don't know why y'all come down here anyway to fight us. Billy Yank, we never done you no hurt, did we?"

If Danny'd been around to talk to, I might not have drifted out to the barn where those graycoats were penned up quite so often. Or maybe he would have made some sense out of what had happened. Things being as they were, all I could do was nod to the rebs and scribble notes to Ma and Pa, my brother and sisters. I wrote Ollie, too, hoping his pa would send the letter along if Ollie'd gone back to the ranks.

The regiment got fifty fresh men the next week, and Company I's losses were made good. Captain Jayroe introduced me to our new drummer, a long-legged fifteen-year-old named Tom Hitchcock.

"See he learns the calls," the captain said. "And you and Tom can pair up shelter halves. Be great friends, the two of you."

I knew he was thinking it would be like with Danny. It wasn't. I tried to teach the drumming, figuring since Danny taught me I owed a debt. Tom was slow to frustration, and he didn't take to following directions from a mite of a boy like me.

"Don't you go to orderin' me 'round, Powell!" Tom barked.

"I'm a head taller than you, and I'm able to bash you proper if I've got a mind."

"You got a mind, have a try," I said, squaring off with both fists bared.

We had at it then. I guess it was bound to happen, but I was sorry for it after. I'd been mad since Droop Mountain, and poor Hitchcock just wound up crosswise to my meanness. I was a regular bobcat that day, and before I was through Hitchcock was in need of Surgeon Blair's attentions, and I was pretty fair dusted off myself.

We weren't the only ones fighting. Trouble was breaking out all over. Men got rankled over card games or quarreled over guard duty. Colonel Harris read the sour mood of his regiment and ordered extra furloughs for Christmas. He also pried six months' pay out of the paymaster.

I'm not sure who was happier to see that money—us or the merchants of western Virginia. Once they took off such assessments as had been made against my thirteen dollars a month, I still had fifty-two dollars left. I sent ten home and spent thirty getting myself outfitted in a fine new woolen uniform. A Beverly tailor actually stitched the cloth so it fit, and I had a good pair of boots, too.

"You look like a real soldier, R. J.," Red proclaimed when I showed off my new duds. "Fit to sing for the general's mess."

And before the season was over, I did just that. Hoping to patch up ill feelings, I brought along battered Tom Hitchcock, but his voice was mostly croak, and he contented himself beating a drum.

The coming of the new year found Company I spread out around Petersburg, combing the countryside for bushwhackers again. My new woolens proved welcome, for the weather went from bad to worse. Nights were freezing in those mountains, and we were alternately smothered by snow and assailed by hail.

On the third day of January 1864, Captain Jayroe got orders to provide an escort for a supply column.

"Fresh shot and powder for the real fightin'," Red grumbled when Lieutenant Ahem began counting off twenty-one volunteers.

"Best take Powell there with you, too," the captain advised. "You could need a drummer, and I believe the trip would do him some good."

"Yes, sir," I said, grinning with anticipation. We'd be riding in the wagons, after all, and the captain handed me two new wool blankets to help against the cold.

"Watch out for rebs, youngster," Cap said as he helped me up alongside Sam Brooks, atop the lead wagon.

"Best they watch out for him," Sam said. "Eh, Hitch?"

Lord bless him if Tom didn't holler a cheerful "Amen!"

We headed out into a fog-shrouded morning. The wagons led the way, followed by a small herd of cattle. We rolled along the Moorefield road ten miles or so without a hint of trouble. Then I saw three shadowy shapes.

In the fog, you couldn't quite be certain what you were seeing. At first I thought maybe it was a bunch of stray horses. Then, hopefully, Sam suggested it was some of General Averell's cavalry come to add their weight to our escort. But it wasn't.

"Rebs!" Red yelled.

The teamsters lashed their horses and tried to get away, but it was hopeless. The snows had bogged the countryside, and the reb horsemen had the road blocked in both directions. Most of the drivers dropped their lines and ran for the nearest cover.

"Beat that drum, R. J.," Red howled as he jumped down and worked at ramming a charge down his rifle. Sam shoved me off the wagon and tossed me my drum, and I beat assembly. Lieutenant Ahem was barking orders, but wasn't a one of them to be understood. It was happening too quickly. When the rebs charged, we took to our heels. It was a regular race. We all of us scattered. I was with Sam and Jim Dyer, stumbling in the snow, when a pistol shot punctured my drum. A big reb sloshed past, splattering us with mud as he knocked Sam to the ground. Dyer threw down his rifle and raised his hands, but I kept going twenty feet or so before a cavalry lieutenant raced along, grabbed me by the arm, and pulled me up across his saddle, knocking the breath out of me.

"Growin' Yanks small these days," the lieutenant declared as he waved his hand in the air and collected his raiders. In less than ten minutes the battle of Moorefield Junction was over. Our whole escort was grabbed, together with the wagons. Our little band was disarmed, thrown in the back of two wagons, and dragged to a nearby town. There, amid howls of celebration, the rebs handed out the captured supplies and slaughtered steers.

We stood around, gazing in disbelief at our fate. Twenty reb guards stared at us over the long barrels of their muskets while a raggedy captain decided what to do with us. Then a tall fellow with the bushiest beard I ever saw rode up. The rebs shouted a greeting. One young graycoat, noticing our confusion, shouted, "Have yourselves a good look, Yanks! That's General Fitzhugh Lee himself!"

And so we learned the worst. We hadn't been nabbed by a band of irregulars sure to parole us home or give our regiment a chance to retake us. No, it wasn't even ragtag horsemen like Colonel Jackson's boys who'd fought us on Droop Mountain. We'd come up against the cream of the reb army! General Bob Lee's own nephew had grabbed off a chunk of Company I.

"See they're fed and dispatch them to Staunton," the general instructed. "Send all the wagons and bring back supplies from the depot. Find ten men for an escort, Captain. Once you're in Staunton, turn them over to the local people and get a receipt."

"Looks like you boys get to ride to Staunton," the captain then told us. "Courtesy of the U.S. Army. From there it's warmth and comfort till the train comes. I envy y'all. You'll be in Richmond 'fore the week's out."

"Richmond," Sam said. "I never once been there, and I've lived in Virginia all my life."

"I've never even ridden a train," I told him. "Guarded a few."

"Be a regular adventure," Jimmy Dyer added.

"No, it won't," the reb guard said, spitting tobacco juice at our feet. "Be Libby Prison for you boys. 'Less they get to exchangin' prisoners again. Ain't a dog I'd wish into that place."

Red shuddered, and I turned even paler than normal. Lieutenant Ahem urged us not to worry, as we weren't in Staunton yet.

"Averell's got patrols sweeping the Shenandoah Valley," he boasted. "Probably has his whole brigade camped in Staunton this minute."

The rebs just laughed. As things turned out, they were a

far sight better informed than our young lieutenant. We were the rest of that day and all night on the road. We arrived in Staunton early in the morning and were turned over to a murderous-looking lot of rascals down by the railhead. A reb major took personal charge of the lieutenant, but the rest of us were marched to a small freight warehouse, together with a dozen or so other prisoners rounded up here and there.

"Howdy, Yanks," a big rawboned fellow said as we formed two lines. "You boys been fresh outfitted, and likely paid, too. We Southern patriots have to make do on short rations and scant pay. 'Less we come into good fortune like today, that is."

The rebs produced pistols and grinned. I half thought they'd shoot us then and there. Instead, they ordered us to peel ourselves while they searched us and our clothes for guns and money.

There wasn't a particle of heat in that warehouse, and when I discarded my blankets, the cold gripped me. Once out of my woolens, I near danced with chills. My teeth beat a tune, and every inch of me broke out in goose bumps.

"Lordy, what luck," a little reb fellow declared as he snatched my new boots. Another one stole my blankets, but the little one grabbed my pants, shirt, and even my drawers. "Got close to twenty Union dollars here, too!"

"That'd be mine," a rough-looking sergeant said, taking the money. "Andy, we can't haul him to Richmond bone naked. You best leave him your flannel shirt and them trousers."

The reb happily stripped and left me his rags in place of my fine new outfit. I felt like crying, seeing him decked out in that tunic, with my shiny brass buttons. The reb even stole my cap.

"Can't be helped," Red whispered as he gripped my shoulders.

"Here, boy," Johnny Poland said, tossing me his wool nightshirt. "Not much to make up the loss, but it's warm."

"Better'n a dress!" the little reb cackled. "Ain't much to you, is there, Billy Yank?"

"Set aside your pistol and see for yourself," I answered with blazing eyes.

He grinned at the notion for a minute. I was breathing fire, though, and it unsettled him some. Weren't many of my companions happy just then, either, and we were a whisper away from charging those thieves. I might have led the way except I noticed how the others were giving up pocket watches, gold lockets with wives' or sweethearts' pictures, hand-me-downs, and keepsakes right and left. I slipped the nightshirt over my bony shoulders and got into the reb's rags. Wasn't an hour later they marched us out onto a platform and loaded us in a Virginia Central Railroad boxcar.

"Enjoy the trip, Yanks!" the thieving sergeant shouted, waving a gold watch at us while his men nailed the door shut.

And so we started the long journey to Richmond.

Up to that point, I don't think I'd ever been really, shook-down-to-the-bone scared in all my life. Being small had gotten me into the habit of scrapping my way along, and I'd found out it was better to bite my lip and snarl a hair than run and hide. But huddling there in that cold, dark boxcar was something new. Even at Droop Mountain Danny'd been close by, and when the worst came, it happened quick. Now there we were, crammed together like cordwood, not knowing what awaited us, with only the whining of metal wheels straining against iron rails to drown out our coughs and sobs.

"Hunker yourself down here alongside us, R. J.," Red Armhult urged when light began to penetrate cracks in the wooden frame of the boxcar.

"Sure, we'll look after you," Poland agreed. The others sort of formed a circle around me, rubbing my hands to keep them warm or swapping a story sure to raise a laugh.

"Ain't nothin' to worry yerself over this trip," Red told me. "Others've made it before, and more are certain to follow."

"Sure," Sam Brooks agreed as he wrapped an icy arm around my shivering shoulders. "Go ahead and have yourself a cry, though. Them boots was worth sheddin' a tear over. Infernal rebs! Don't leave a body his drawers even!"

Sam clasped my hand and stuffed my fingers through the holes in his new rebel shirt. I couldn't help laughing, and it warmed me.

"Do that some more, Ranny," Poland suggested. A month before I would have scowled at any of them save Danny calling me that. Just then it cheered them thinking me a child to be looked after, and they, helpless as babes, my protectors.

From Staunton we headed eastward. The train stopped every so often, and sometimes we were marched off a ways and given some cornbread to eat. In Charlottesville we got a cup of hot pea soup. The rebs also emptied the waste buckets and filled our water barrel. Later we were whole hours without stopping, and Johnny Poland pried some boards loose so we could empty those buckets along the way. The smell improved considerably thereafter.

The train stopped a full four hours at a place called Hanover Junction, and we were marched off like prize horses to be shown around the town. Our guards were boys from a military academy, and for once I wasn't the smallest soldier to be seen. I swear a few of those boys had trouble holding onto their muskets.

"Wouldn't be anything to knock those youngsters aside and make a run for cover," Red whispered.

"Get yourself shot," Poland argued. "I know this school. Atwell's turned out its share of brass-button colonels. Those boys can shoot straight, and even if you got clear, you'd just freeze. Our army's a way up north of here."

"Quiet there, Yank!" a little reb barked. "You got the urge to take a try at us, go ahead. They won't let us join up with the real fightin' yet, but I might just plug me a Yankee anyhows."

I thought back to bold talk I'd heard in our camp before Droop Mountain. Before Danny and Maggs got killed. Before I knew what a dead man looked like.

"You wouldn't enjoy it much," I told the young graycoats. "Isn't what you think."

They grinned until they looked deeper into my eyes. Something they saw chilled them.

We were bound back to the depot when a little brown-haired lady wrapped up in a lace shawl dashed right through the Atwell guards, broke our ranks, and grabbed me by the arm.

"Lordy, child, by what odd circumstance have you fallen in with these rogues!" she cried. "You could be my dear dead Freddie sure as I live. Am I right, Grandma?"

A toothless old woman now stepped out of the shadows, nodding her head and gumming out some rebel muddle. In her arms were a smallish brown coat and a patchwork quilt.

"Ma'am, you'd best stand aside," a sad-faced corporal ordered.

"Nonsense," the lady answered. "You don't mean to send this child barefoot and half-naked into winter confinement. Here, boy, take these to fight the cold," the lady said, passing first the quilt and later the coat into my arms. "Get Albert's hat, too," she ordered, and the granny rushed into a nearby house and returned with a fine embroidered kepi, blue bordered with red top. "My husband's," she told me. "With the artillery till Sharpsburg."

I nodded as she placed the oversized cap onto my head. She slipped my arms into the coat, and Red wrapped the quilt around me. Three other ladies then arrived carrying cups of hot cider. They passed among us, offering their warm drinks.

"We don't wish you ill, Yankees," one of the newcomers said. "We only wish you home."

"I wish it myself," Sam said, grinning.

"We thank you," Poland told the women. "Let's have a cheer for them, boys!"

We raised a howl, and the Atwell boys added a second.

"Well, Red Cap," Sam said, slapping my back. "If we can just find you some shoes you might live to see spring."

"I'll live," I said, shaking off the melancholy—and adopting my new name.

We arrived in Richmond a hair shy of dawn the tenth day of January 1864. Our train chugged to a halt on the far side of a long bridge, and a detachment of guards promptly tore the nails from the boxcar door and led us out into the crisp, cool air.

"Line up in twos, Yanks!" a burly sergeant growled. We did as ordered and soon found ourselves marching through the streets alongside the river, past warehouses and levees. Already the street showed activity. Small groups of men in uniform walked by. A carriage swept past in a hurry. The guards pointed out the massive marble capitol building, with its statue of George Washington. Thomas Jefferson designed the place, one soldier boasted.

"Washington and Jefferson, who would have held with our cause. Southern rights, hurrah!" the reb sergeant called.

The people in the street paid him no mind, and we shuffled along in our bare feet, hoping it wouldn't be too much farther. That was one wish not granted, for we trudged along for what seemed an eternity. Finally, footsore and bone weary, we arrived at a massive warehouse. There was a sign over the door, reading THOMAS LIBBY & SONS, SHIP CHANDLERS AND GROCERS."

"Libby Prison," Red whispered.

I recalled a dozen tales of horror told of the place and shuddered.

"We be takin' good care o' you Yanks here," the sergeant told us as the door swung open.

"And we'll tend to you fellows a bit later," Poland promised him.

Once we were led into the prison proper, though, we made no more boasts. The long captivity was about to begin. And all we could see around us was grim, heartless death.

6

Libby Prison was a nightmare. We were herded like cattle into a large room and again subjected to the humiliation of being stripped and robbed. Some of the men had managed to hide bits of money in their hair or elsewhere. One fellow stuffed silver coins in his ears. The guards at Libby knew every place a copper could hide, and they combed every last penny from our wretched bodies. They picked at our clothes, but when one of them made a move on my quilt, I had a coughing fit.

"What's wrong with you, li'l Yank?" the guard asked.

"He's had a skirmish with the pox," Red Armhult answered.

"Lordy, keep yer blanket, youngster. Got no interest in pox," the guard declared.

They ordered us to dress, then marched us to another room.

"That li'l 'un's got the pox, doc," our guard exclaimed.

The reb doc walked over and looked me over. He unbuttoned my new coat and had a look at my chest. Then he ran his hands along my arms. When he got to my vaccination scar, he grinned.

"Pox, huh?" he whispered. He made a great show then of pinching my arms and tapping his fingers against my chest. "You've some fluid in your lungs, son," he told me. "Get some fresh air if you can and see you boil your water. Wish I had a pair of shoes for you," he added as he buttoned up my coat. "I don't know what's got into men, locking away children. If it was my say-so, I'd send you home today."

It wasn't, so he did the next best thing. He saw I got a blanket to wrap around my feet. Two days later he brought me a stick of candy to lick.

"Sugar can't hurt the pox," he said, laughing.

"Boy, sugar's worth its weight in silver in Richmond," one of the guards told me later.

"Then why . . ."

"Doc lost his youngest boy on Culp's Hill, with Dick Ewell," the guard explained. "Makes the fourth one gone. You favor the lad some, I guess."

"Tell him—"

"Thank him your own self," the guard said, giving me a shove that sent me sprawling. I stared up in surprise and only softened when I noticed the cussed sergeant watching. Even the friendliest reb'd wallop you when that devil three-striper happened along.

The old-timers at Libby welcomed us grimly. They were happy to have news of the war, but they had only grave tidings for us.

"Many a man's died at Libby," an Illinois cavalryman told me. "Twenty, thirty every day, we hear. But at least Libby's got a roof. Over at Belle Isle there's just open ground."

"Fresh air and plenty of water there," a Michigan man

pointed out. "I could use my blanket for a roof. Have before."

I guess Red Armhult pretty much summed up Libby when we had our own chance to greet a band of newcomers.

"Howdy, boys," Red called. "Welcome to hell."

I recalled Mr. Havers telling us the old Greeks believed that down in Hades you were doomed to the worst possible fate. If you feared snakes, you'd have them crawling all over you. Or if you hated darkness, you'd never see a hint of light. Well, no Greek could have thought up a place to top the Hotel Libby, as some of the men called it. You barely had room to scratch, and what with graybacks—lice—swarming everywhere, there was plenty of need. It was quite a sight when a prisoner died. Those graybacks evacuated the corpse like a miniature army.

In the room where I was shut up, it never got warm. Most mornings I awoke to find my breath forming clouds of mist. We were packed tight against one another at night, and the warmth of others' bodies was the sole thing that prevented us from freezing solid. We were forbidden to approach the windows for fear we might be signaling phantom armies to the north, and the air was an abomination. The rebs did send slaves in to scrub the floors every once in a while, but there was no scrubbing ourselves. We almost never had enough drinking water, and nobody was about to waste any on bathing.

"If I was to wash my clothes," Poland declared, "they'd out and out dissolve. Only the dirt's keepin' 'em together."

As for food, the rebs concocted a sort of black bean soup that they fed us regular, together with squares of cornbread. The bread was coarse and hard to chew, but the soup was amazing. I once counted twelve beans in one bowl—and thirty-seven bugs.

"Takes forever to pick out the mites," Red grumbled.

"Don't do it," Poland advised. "They're sort of crunchy."

We occupied ourselves playing cards or talking about the war. First on everybody's mind was the rumored resumption of the exchange, meaning we'd be swapped for a batch of rebs. Gambling followed a close second. Men would make their own decks of cards using writing paper. Everything from a grandfather's watch to woolen drawers were wagered. A favorite affair was cockroach wrestling. Next to that came all sorts of bug races.

Johnny Poland had a champion cricket for ten days. That insect would line up, and Poland would put a hot match to its tail. Lord, but that hopper close to flew. Then one time Poland lit the poor thing on fire, and the champ racer of Libby Prison had itself a Viking funeral.

Because of his good fortune wagering, Poland managed to store up a bit of cash, not to mention odds and ends of food and equipment. Mostly these came from relatives who sent packages to their captured loved ones. I never once saw a letter from my home while at Richmond, but I often impersonated this dead boy or that in order to get the packages sent them. For my trouble I'd get a few coins, but the real reward was enjoying the watchful attentions of my elders. I returned their favors with singing.

"Red Cap!" the men would often call. "Red Cap!" And I would offer up some old hymn or camp tune.

I guess it was around the end of January, when we'd been at Libby three weeks, that I began to notice myself changed. The old hardness that had always been in my legs had turned to mush. My elbows and knees began to stretch my skin. Some of the others were losing teeth and hair. Bright light caused us to flinch.

There never had been all that much of me, but now I was just melting away. The rebs had stolen my suspenders, and the belt they'd left me wasn't capable of keeping my britches up. Sam Brooks had a needle, though, and he punched me some new holes through the leather. Still, it was unsettling to know that there I was, headed for fifteen and showing hints of getting taller when the rest of me was growing out and out narrow.

"Sorry I've no more sugar to feed you, Red Cap," the reb doctor told me the first week of February. "But word is you won't any of you be here much longer. Pray the exchange is resumed, son. Pray it with all your heart."

I did—three, four times each day. I prayed for exchange in the same breath that I cursed black beans and graybacks and no shoes. And each day that passed, the living in Libby got worse, and the dying were set beside the door in ever-growing numbers.

"Don't go to fadin' on us, R. J.," Red scolded the day I refused to get up to fetch my ration.

"What else can I do?" I asked. "I'm sick of moldy meal and bad soup. I'm hungry. I ache all over. I miss my family—and Danny and clouds and birds and running."

"I know," he said, lifting me up like a stick of wood and resting me on his angular shoulder. "It's a crime to pen a boy up with all these flea-bitten rascals. But you got a duty to hold up your spirits, son. You're our drummer. Mascot, too. We look to you to set the pace, remember?"

"Danny was better at it."

"Danny Hays was a prankster and a first-rate rogue, but he never brought the men to cheer like you did. Have you forgotten old Maggs? He rushed right into the jaws of death to snatch you from harm."

"Better he'd stayed with the company," I grumbled.

"I've had about all of this I'll stomach, Powell," he said, setting me down a moment, then throwing me across his knee and giving me a hard whack across the bottom. There wasn't much flesh there, and it caused a considerable *thwack*.

"Red, you've lost your senses!" Poland yelled, racing over to pry me from the madman's grasp.

"They're hurtin' Red Cap!" somebody hollered. Before I knew what had happened, half a hundred men set upon Red, and I was carried to safety by fifteen hands.

"Don't hurt him!" I shouted as I scrambled to my feet. "Don't!"

"Boy's lost his senses," one fellow declared. "Why, he was beatin' you, sonny."

"No!" I yelled, jumping into the middle of the melee and rescuing Red from his attackers. "Got yourself battered a mite," I declared when I examined Red's swollen face.

"Worse'n that, R. J.," Red said, grinning. "Near busted my hand on your rump. You're all bones, boy!"

Once the others saw we were on good terms, they left us to mend fences and returned to their square of floor.

"I guess it worked, didn't it?" I asked. "Not feeling so sorry for myself anymore."

"You got cause to," Red admitted. "Only it don't help. You have to keep fightin' 'em, R. J. Every inch. Promise me you will."

"I will," I vowed.

It wasn't long afterward a company of rebs appeared at Libby to escort one whole mess from the prison.

"Won't keep anybody but officers here now," one of the guards explained.

"Where are they taking us?" I asked.

"Not to Belle Isle," the guard answered. "No, they'd be headin' th'other way. Depot, I'd guess."

"To be exchanged?"

"Not as I heard, but then I'm not General Lee nor Jefferson Davis either one. Could be they've gone and grown some sense, even that drunkard Grant."

"Grant?" I asked, wondering what he had to do with it.

"It's him's stopped the exchange," a reb corporal told us. "Says it favors our cause. Swappin' a man for a man? How's that favor us?"

I hoped Grant might have changed his mind. It certainly seemed so, for not long afterward the rebs announced our mess was leaving Libby.

"Know where we're bound to?" we asked near anyone within earshot. "Has the exchange started up again?"

"Don't know," the guards answered. "Be a crowd o' celebratin' boys both sides of the lines if it has, though."

Just the thought of it had us marching double time to the depot.

"We're goin' home," one or another of us mumbled out loud.

Lord, that word sounded good. Home. I could taste Ma's plum puddings, could smell pumpkin bread in the oven.

The rebs crammed us into three boxcars, and the train surged into motion. We rode only twenty or thirty miles, though, before we were marched back onto a platform.

"This the exchange point?" a Michigan sergeant asked. "When will we be leaving?"

"Exchange?" a freckled corporal asked.

68

"Aren't we headed north?" Red asked.

"Naw," the corporal explained as a squad of smartly dressed infantry appeared. "You boys headed south. Georgia way."

A snail could have crushed the lot of us. We were more than just disappointed. Our new guards nodded sympathetically. They stood by while we got a bit of cornbread and some water into us.

"Georgia's a long way, Yanks," a one-armed captain said. "Give your legs a stretch on the platform. We'll take ten at a time off to the trees yonder."

I don't suppose you could say there was any love in that captain's eyes for us, but I read respect there. It was something I was learning fast. We always got better treatment from soldiers who'd been on the field of battle. We'd been robbed and bullied by those stay-behinds. This batch, who turned out to be part of General George Pickett's command, resting up after their failed charge at Gettysburg, didn't feed us sugar candy, but they did give us some space to lie down and allowed us our fill of water.

By and by a train pulled onto the tracks alongside the platform, and the reb captain got us lined up. Doors were thrown open, and we were stuffed into the confines of a boxcar once again. Lately that car had hauled tobacco, and some of the boys had a high time gathering up scraps of leaves to chew on the journey. Better still, there were large gaps between the boards, and we could stare out at the surrounding countryside. We had air to breathe, too.

"We'll be prisoners a time yet, eh, Red?" I asked as he sat beside me.

"Till spring anyway, I'd judge," he grumbled.

"I'll be fifteen before I see my family again," I told him.

"We'll have to be thinking up something to do for your birthday, R. J.," Sam declared. "You know I thought you was a bit taller. Feared I was shrinkin' at first, but now I think of it . . ."

"He's right, boy," Poland told me. "Edgin' past halfway to five feet. Any whiskers?"

I touched my chin, but it was smooth as ever. They laughed, and I started to lash out at them. The car rolled into motion, though, and my words were lost in the screech of the wheels straining against the rails.

7

We were down in Raleigh in the Carolinas when the train next stopped. We were near choked from confinement and cross to boot. Worse, we were given a company of militia for guards. They marched us to a stand of timber and spread us out in a loose circle.

"You boys sit yourselves down and stay down," their captain told us. "Any man stands before daybreak, one of my boys'll see he don't ever rise again."

"Aren't we goin' to be fed?" somebody asked.

"You Yank devils don't merit favors," the captain yelled. "But we'll feed you. Now get yourselves flat!"

"Ain't been travelin' in high style, Johnny," our spokesman went on. "Many a man's got a nature call to tend."

"Ten minutes," the captain replied. "We'll take you to the trees in pairs. Any man wanders, he dies."

A sharp report three minutes later was followed by a cry, and we knew that captain had kept his word. The militia didn't go out of their way to feed us, either. I got two stale crackers and some mint tea. I could feel the empty knot in my stomach tighten.

Just before dusk a Boston fellow made a sort of map in the sandy ground, and we traced out our journey.

"Just where's Georgia?" Red asked me. "You're an educated fellow, R. J. Where's she lie?"

"Down here," I said, marking the state by putting in the South Carolina and Florida boundaries.

"That's a long way still, ain't it?" Sam Brooks asked.

" 'Bout as deep into Dixie as a man can get," the Bostonian noted.

" 'Fore this is all over, be many of us deeper," a sandy-haired corporal said. "Lyin' molderin' in our graves like ole John Brown."

He was right, too. Before morning the reb militia shot three. Two forgot the order and stood up during the night. The third made a run for it. He got a hundred yards before three shots brought his escape to an end.

I didn't hold it against those rebs for shooting. They had their job, after all. But afterward they laughed and taunted us to try some more. That rankled us all. If we'd had an ounce of strength among us, we'd have charged that band of devils and settled accounts. But scarecrows were a poor match for muskets.

We went without breakfast, too. The guards were getting their fill of bread and bacon, but they failed to share. A town boy did bring us a few buckets of water.

"What's in Georgia?" I asked him.

"How'd I know?" the reb said, chewing a straw. "I never been out of Carolina."

It wasn't long before I found myself wedged in the back

corner of a boxcar again, squeezed against Red Armhult's side and bouncing off Johnny Poland's elbow.

"Georgia, huh?" I muttered.

"Can't be worse'n Libby," someone declared. "Or this boxcar, either."

"Pray they ain't got black beans down thataways," Poland suggested.

"Amen," we cried in a chorus.

The train got to moving then, and the groans of the car and the whine of the wheels gnawed at our empty bellies. Thereafter we chugged along a few hours, then piled out of the cars for some air. We ate some, slept some, and prayed we were close to the end of our journey.

Late on the twenty-seventh we reached Macon, Georgia.

"Ain't far now," our guards announced. "Past Americus."

"I been there," one man told us, nodding hopefully. "Good country. Woods, water, farms all around. Fruits and vegetables."

It made my head spin to think of it, but deep down I wouldn't be cheered. Every mile we traveled was a mile farther from home.

It was around midnight when the train pulled to a stop at a small siding. Once we climbed onto the platform and adjusted our eyes, we discovered we were in the middle of flat, empty country. A sign over a small hut read ANDERSON STATION.

"Line yourselves up, Yanks," a voice boomed. A row of pitch pine torches were lit, and we found ourselves stumbling down a quarter mile of dusty road. We were then led to a gate in a tall palisade of pine poles.

"Spread out, boys," the guards told us. "We're bound to search you."

We were used to stripping for the amusement of the rebs by now, and we hardly even grumbled. In the faint light I saw just how thin my companions had grown, though, and I had the first real good look at myself since leaving the Libby Hotel.

"Sorry, Billy Yank," a guard said as I pried the filthy strips of blanket from my feet.

"Sorry myself," I replied. "Got nothing left to steal."

"No need to peel yourself bare," he said when I started to drop my drawers. "Appears to me you had enough such handling for a time."

I gazed up at him with surprise. He was maybe twenty-five, tall and lean, and he handed me my shirt with a good-natured grin.

"Thanks, sir," I told him as I slipped the rag over my shoulders.

Shortly thereafter we were marched inside the stockade. Red pulled me along to a piece of unoccupied ground, and the rest of Company I spread itself nearby. I curled up in my quilt and fell into a deep sleep.

8

The sun woke us. I rubbed the sleep from my eyes and stood up to find myself surrounded by a sea of groggy prisoners. We, in turn, were nearly encircled by a wall of pine logs two to three inches in diameter and more than twenty feet high. Those logs were set alongside each other so close we couldn't catch even a hint of what lay beyond. Every few feet there stood a guard's roost. The palisade wasn't finished, though, and along the open side we glimpsed a sort of earthwork between us and a forest of tall pines.

"Listen here, you new Yanks!" a rebel sergeant barked at us. "Form up in lines and get counted off. Now!"

We did as ordered.

"Now, keep watch over your gear," the sergeant warned. Other prisoners were eyeing our pitiful blankets already, and I threw my quilt over one shoulder. The reb sergeant then counted us off in lots of one hundred. "Fer drawin' rations," he explained.

We further divided ourselves into messes of twenty-five.

The twenty of us from Company I took in five other West Virginians. When the ration wagon rolled through the gate, we were meted out a quart of coarse cornmeal, a sweet potato, and a few ounces of salted beef—each!

"We're in clover, boys!" Johnny Poland exclaimed.

Red Armhult, who took charge on account of his two stripes, assigned Sam Brooks to oversee the cooking up of our cornbread. One of our new messmates managed to acquire a skillet in exchange for a spare blanket, and the rest of us hurried to collect branches and logs that were scattered about the compound to use as firewood.

"Save the long ones for poles," a veteran of the camp advised. We did just that. While Sam and his little party set about cooking our rations, I paired up with Red to construct a tent of sorts out of his blanket. I managed to rig lines out of cloth strips and Red traded some of his buttons to the reb guards for twine and old shoelaces. By nightfall we'd assembled a dozen makeshift shelters. Some we covered with blankets or canvas. One or two of the boys had their rubber blankets along, and those did the job even better. We used thatched pine branches to cover the rest.

Those shebangs, as they were called, were poor shelter, and I doubted they'd be of much use in a real rain. Just the same it improved our spirits, knowing we had some kind of home.

Once we had our shelters up, we set about exploring the prison proper. The place had two gates, one on either side of Sweetwater Branch, a sluggish sort of stream that provided our drinking and bathing water. It also washed the drainage from the sinks out of the prison. In those early days, the water was clean enough. I didn't waste a lot of time before half drowning myself there. It was a popular spot, for all the

Richmond boys were infested with graybacks, and the only way to shed them was to drown them or die. I chose the first option.

I did my best to get the filth off my clothes, too, but lacking soap I only lightened them up some. My trousers just about disintegrated, and I wound up using what was left of the legs to patch the rest. I looked like a boy in knee pants, and my companions had a good hoot about that.

"Take care o' them britches, Red Cap," some Ohioans in the next mess shouted. "Next thing you know you'll be wearin' a diaper."

"At least I won't be from Ohio," I hollered at them. "Must be a frightful burden to bear, that!"

After my bath and the mending, I drifted out to where the rebs were putting up the new stockade logs. There were two hundred Negroes building that wall—hacking off pine bark from the poles or using ropes to set them in holes five feet deep. I'd never seen that many slaves in all my life, and it seemed strange to me they should wind up making a jail for the very folks who'd come south to fight for their freedom.

Must have seemed odd to them, too. Of course, they didn't have any choice. They didn't hurry the work along, and if you really listened to the slow, mournful songs they sang, they'd throw in a hint or two of their feelings. They also managed to drop ears of corn or stack peas and carrots where we'd find them. The food was welcome, but it was the kindness we most appreciated.

That first week I learned a bit about our new home. The rebs named it Camp Sumter, I suppose after the fort where the whole business got started. We took to calling it Andersonville, after the nearby town. Or maybe just to spite the rebs. We tended toward contrariness in those days. We also had our first look at the man in charge, General John H. Winder.

Winder! Any Marylander would recognize the name. His papa was a general, too—the one who took to his heels at Bladensburg and gave the British a chance to burn Washington in 1814. The reb guards called him the Confederacy's "bedroom spy." He was provost general, a sort of chief of police for the army, and he spent his time watching Richmond ladies instead of fighting us.

You couldn't help noticing Winder. He waddled around the stockade, barking orders and cussing anybody who got in his way. I was down at the sinks one day when he happened by. His eyes drifted down onto my back, and I sensed something evil was about to tap me on the shoulder.

"What you looking at, boy?" he shouted when I turned and stared.

Not much, I thought.

I dipped my head and headed off to my shebang. Better not to rile generals, whether they wore blue or gray. Ole Winder had a laugh as I went.

"Don't they have any full-sized soldiers left to send south?" he taunted.

"Don't pay him any mind," Red told me. "Who ever had any use for gen'rals!"

Anyway, we had more exciting business to witness. That night a band of prisoners tossed a knotted line over the stockade. It caught in a notch, and they climbed up one at a time. I guess fifteen or so made it—right past the reb guard's camp! Or so we thought. A rifle shot told us otherwise. They didn't even make it past shouting distance before they were rounded up. Next morning the rebs led the would-be escapers back, their ankles shackled to iron balls.

"Best you Yanks learn to content yourselves with our hospitality," the sergeant who brought the ration wagon warned. "Next 'uns we might just skin like rabbits."

"Ain't natural the way them rebs grabbed off our boys," Johnny Poland remarked afterward.

He was right. We learned later a batch of our own men had sold out the escape.

"Was N'Yawkers," Red told us.

I winced at the news. We'd heard stories of a group of scavengers from the boys confined at Belle Isle. The other prisoners called them New Yorkers, after the leader, who was supposed to be from that state. Those Empire Staters true to the cause claimed otherwise, but the name stuck. The leader was a heartless devil we named Mosby, after the rebel who was famous for raiding and bushwhacking up in Virginia.

"They come your way, all you can do is pray," a Connecticut corporal told me. "They'll beat you silly, then rob everything you got. We had a boy no bigger'n you stripped to the skin and clubbed to boot. Poor fellow's still dizzy."

As if we didn't have problems aplenty, the rebs marked a line twenty feet inside the stockade. They drove stakes in the ground and ran twine between them. Once it was all done, a reb lieutenant explained it.

"What you see there's a deadline," the lieutenant said. "Any man crosses the line gets himself a bullet. Understand?"

If we didn't, the rebs made it clear fast enough. Wasn't two days before a reb guard shot an Indiana boy in the leg, and a bit later, after firing a warning round, the rebs killed an old-timer from some Boston regiment.

"Appears they're serious, don't it?" Red asked me.

"I'd say," I answered.

Thereafter our condition worsened. Each day another train arrived. About five hundred men got off and marched through the gates. Once there were as many as eight hundred—a whole regiment's worth. And the spring hadn't even started.

We began to fall into a sort of daily routine, broken up by a spot of card playing and occasional fistfights. First thing each morning the new prisoners were counted off into messes. It sometimes took hours, and I watched men faint from the exertion of standing in line and waiting their turn. We old-timers, meanwhile, had to wait to get our rations. And so far as food was concerned, it got scarcer and poorer in quality every day.

I gazed at my shrinking flesh and shook my head. But I was luckier than some. I was still alive.

I helped carry one dead fellow to the gate myself. He was stiff as a board, stripped naked, and a horror to lay eyes upon. His big toes were tied together to help ease the carrying, and they'd folded his hands across his chest. Ribs and bones protruded through the sallow flesh, and his eyes stared blankly at the sky.

One of his friends had scribbled the poor man's name and regiment on a scrap of paper and hung it around his neck.

"They might have spared him a shirt," Red grumbled.

"Needed for the living, I guess," I said, grudging his messmates for robbing him and leaving him for others to carry to the gate. "Wish I had my drum so I could play taps for him."

80

"Be a comfort, no doubt," Red said as we laid the body alongside another. "For him and the rest that's sure to follow."

I nodded, and when he pulled me over to his side as we walked back to our shebang, I leaned on him some. It was a comfort, Red's big hand on my shoulder. I wished I could have thought up some prank to bring on his friendly grin.

By March we'd come to be veterans of prison. All in all, we'd been locked up somewhere a couple of months by then, and it had taken its toll. Fellows were dying faster—even those who weren't were chasing graves, as Red put it.

Our little company was getting along better than most. We had a good spot for our camp, and fair shelters, having gotten in early. Then, too, Sam proved a good cook, and Jimmy Dyer had a talent for commerce. He'd swap one bunch or another out of all sorts of things. He even got a cake of soap. Some Illinois boys started a well, and then a laundry. Jimmy and Red both helped scrub clothes and picked up a bit of spare food, which they generally shared.

We also carried on a lively lousing business. That was quite a sport. You built a fire and ran clothes over the top. Those little lice popped out of the cloth, just like corn kernels shook in a pan. It was entertaining, and we picked up a few buttons, a crust of bread, or a spare potato in the bargain.

The extra food was welcome. Rations seemed to dwindle daily. As for vegetables, they were scarcer than gold nuggets in Andersonville. Scurvy was plaguing us, and every day I screwed my thumb into my flesh and looked for signs of scurvy. If the skin color changed, you had trouble. Bleeding gums and loose teeth were other signs.

Men were starting to suffer from fevers, too. Red judged water the main cause and warned me to avoid the stream.

"Those Illinois cavalry boys'll share their well. You just ask 'em quiet," Red explained.

The other thing Red got me started on was taking walks. We traced a path through one mess and around another until we covered three miles or so in all. The exercise hardened up the muscles, and the walk gave some purpose to the long days. We occasionally had a game of sorts, tossing around a ball of rags, and a fair portion of the camp threw dice or shot marbles. Those who could find a piece of root or a stick and could trade a reb guard out of a bayonet whittled.

Me, I stayed clear of the gambling. I had no acquaintance with luck. Danny would have owned half the camp, I suppose, but then he was lying on a West Virginia hillside. Anyway, I took my walks and did my best to stay clear of raiders.

That was considerably easier than watching the lines of the dead growing longer.

"Do you figure we'll any of us live to see the outside of this place?" I asked Red one night as he coughed himself to sleep.

"Hope so, R. J. It would bother me some otherwise."

"Me, too," I said, trying to force a grin onto my face. And a bit later, as Sam mopped our corporal's forehead, I sang for my companions, hoping the music would ease their worries.

9

Our high hopes of good treatment at Andersonville faded into disappointment. Our clothes were mere rags, and there was scant hope of any replacements. When we did manage to swap some newcomer out of a blanket for a pair of sticks to use for shebang poles, the raiders often as not managed to steal it when we lined up for roll call. Rations continued to dwindle, and they'd be cut off entirely on the poorest excuse.

I was hungry. No, more than that. I was starving. My fist could plunge into my hollow belly and close to come out the other side. There never had been all that much of me, but what was left threatened to melt away.

Worse, warm weather brought an army of insects to torment us. Mosquitoes as big as sparrows attacked day and night. Deadly centipedes—Confederate cavalry, we called them—stung men to death. Spiders spun webs in the sinks, and if one of them bit you, you'd find an arm or a leg swollen double.

We were so pitiful weak it took exertion to rise for roll

call. Red was too sick to take our daily walk, and I dared not try it alone. Most of the smaller prisoners kept to the shadows lest the raiders fall upon them.

The rebs took advantage of our weakness and promised double rations to any man willing to sign his parole and work for them. A few men who had experience with the railroads signed up to go north to Macon. There were calls for carpenters and blacksmiths.

"Yer pa is a smith, R. J.," Red declared. "Maybe they can make use of you."

"I won't help any reb stretch this war a day longer than it has to be," I vowed. "I mustered same as you, until the rebellion is put down."

"Or until you're dead," he barked. "The one could happen 'fore the other."

Johnny Poland, who was getting better food in return for helping with the Illinois boys' laundry, suggested we join the woodcutters. The rebs let us cut trees and keep some of the wood for our own use. We also carried bodies from the gate to the graveyard a quarter mile or so to the north. I couldn't do that often, as the bodies gave me nightmares afterward, but we did get extra food for the labor, and everyone in the mess who was able took a turn.

Those pitiful scarecrows didn't weigh a sliver of what they had a year before, but for me in my weakened state, just keeping the feet off the ground was a real effort. Poland, being only a few inches shy of six feet and accustomed to hard living, had the heavier part. It rankled him to see me straining, though, and once, when I stumbled over a tree root, he took the body and dragged it along himself. I sat there, sort of bewildered. Then a reb guard marched over.

"I'm with the burying detail," I told him as I struggled to my feet. "I fell, and—"

"Sit yourself down, little Yank," he told me in a heavy drawl. "Ain't come to shoot you. Nor to steal anything, either."

He grinned, and I recognized him as the fellow who had searched us when we arrived.

"I best join the others," I argued.

"Who's givin' the orders hereabouts?" he asked. "What's a child like you doin' in this place anyhow? Ain't old enough to pass for a soldier."

"I lied about my age," I confessed, wondering even as the words leaked out why I was telling him. "But I'm fifteen now, and a veteran of battles. R. J. Powell, Company I, Tenth West Virginia Volunteer Infantry."

"I'm Lewis Jones," he explained. "They call you Red Cap."

"And other things besides," I said, matching his grin.

"Ever beat guard mount?" he asked. "Retreat?"

"I'd be a poor drummer not to. And nobody ever accused me of that."

"How would you like to come along to our camp? The Twenty-sixth Alabama, I mean. Beat the drum. We lost our own drummer to a fever night before last, and we miss the calls."

"I joined an army already."

"Ain't askin' you to stack arms, boy. Just to beat a drum. It'd get you clear of the stockade for a time, and we'd put some food in you."

"What else would I have to do?"

"Nothin' in this world. I give you my word on it."

"Your officers will never abide it."

85

"Lieutenant's my own brother," he said, laughing. "What's it matter to them if one boy's plucked out of this swamp?"

"What's it matter to you?"

"Lord, you got a suspicious nature, Red Cap," he said, shaking his head. "I been with the regiment since '61, fought you blue devils all over Virginia. Marched north till you turned us back hard at Sharpsburg, and near won the war at Gettysburg. Got three scars to prove my devotion to Southern rights. But I never signed anything about makin' war on little children. It carves the heart right out of me to see you boys dyin' away, but at least most o' them others got some size. Come beat our drum, Red Cap."

Poland came back from the burying detail then, and the reb repeated his offer.

"He's a dandy drummer, though a lot of trouble," Poland said. "Go along and beat their drum, Powell. Do you good to breathe some fresh air."

And so that afternoon I beat guard mount for the Twenty-sixth Alabama. Reluctant as I was and still suspicious, I had to admit my fingers hated to let go of the sticks when I was finished. As for the rebs, they gave me near half their supper.

"Maybe you'd like to sign a parole and come stay out here with us," Lewis suggested.

"I signed something already," I answered. "Pledged my-self to serve out the war."

"Still aim to see us beat, eh?"

"Not with the same heart as I had once," I confessed. "Not since Droop Mountain when I buried my friend."

"But you're bound to stay true to your word, Red Cap."

"It's about all I got left, Lewis."

86

I swallowed hard as I handed back the drum. He nodded, and the other Alabamans hurried off to a small thatched shed. They returned with some turnips and parsnips, stuffed in a flour sack. Then Lewis escorted me to the north gate and inside till he was satisfied I was in the hands of my friends.

"Wouldn't care to hear you happened by them N'Yawkers," he said, winking. "Watch yourself, son."

Then he turned and marched back to the gate.

"So?" Red asked, eyeing the sack. "Poland said you was captured all over again."

"Went to beat their drum," I said, pulling out a turnip. "They aren't all that bad, those boys."

"No, we ain't suffered so much at their hands as from our own," Poland declared as he helped himself to a parsnip. "Powell, you brought back treasure. Sam, get a fire goin'. We got to brew these up proper."

We made a turnip-parsnip soup, and every man in our mess had a cup or two. Those who looked to need more got it.

"How come you to return, R. J.?" Red asked me after I related my adventure.

"Why haven't you signed a parole yourself?" I asked. "You never expected me to hide from Fitz Lee's cavalry. Why would you think I wouldn't share the trouble now?"

" 'Cause we're all of us dyin' bit by bit," he answered. "And these rebs seem of a sort to treat you right."

I didn't argue. Couldn't. It wasn't something I could explain, how deep down I felt my duty, and signing a parole was no more possible than pulling my backbone out. Wouldn't either one leave me whole.

Likely there wasn't another man in Georgia would have

made me a second offer, but Lewis Jones did. He came into the stockade with the ration wagon one morning and introduced his brother, Lieutenant John W. Jones.

"I won't sign a parole," I announced.

"You don't have to," Lewis explained. "All you got to do is promise me face to face you won't run away."

"I don't understand," I said.

"We need a drummer," the lieutenant told me. "Well?"

"All I have to do is beat the drum?"

"You'll stay in our camp, share our mess," Lewis explained. "Long as we're at Camp Sumter. If we're ordered back to the fighting, well, I can't say you won't have to return inside. But your honor's safe. We'll not ask you to turn from your pledge."

Red, Sam, and Poland all heard. They shouted encouragement, and Poland heaved me onto one shoulder and offered to carry me to their camp.

"Well, Red Cap?" Lieutenant Jones asked.

"Guess I'm bound to go," I answered.

Poland set me down, and Lewis led me toward the gate. It was only that night, after beating out a solemn taps, that I learned from the lieutenant about my special parole.

"Don't you break your promise to my little brother," the officer said. "Lew's got more heart than sense, and he's told the colonel he'll vouch for you. If you were to escape, poor Lew'd answer for it."

"Answer for it?" I asked, wrinkling my forehead.

"They'd shoot him," the lieutenant said, shaking as he spoke the words. And I knew it was the truth.

"Don't worry," I assured him. "I never break a promise."

"Good boy," he said, patting my back. "We're all of us a sort of family, here in the Twenty-sixth. Brothers by bond of fire. And cold and damp. Hunger. You're one of us now, and welcome."

"Thanks," I said.

And so it was I found myself drumming for the Alabamans. As it happened, Lewis was assigned to Company I of the Twenty-sixth, and I took the coincidence for a sign. I joined Lewis, the lieutenant, and a trio of other Alabamans in a mess, though in the beginning they tended to dole out a double portion of everything to me. Inside the stockade we'd imagined those guards feasting on roast pork or boiled beef. Instead I discovered the food as poor outside as in. The difference was the Twenty-sixth was a band of natural-born scroungers, and they were forever shooting rabbits, snagging fish from some creek, or digging wild onions and turnips from the countryside.

My second night with the rebs, I showed them how we roasted lice over a fire. The things popped and sizzled, much to the amusement of my new messmates.

"Lord, Johnny, would you look to this boy's shoulders," Lewis declared, pointing to the small red circles left by burrowing lice.

"Near bad as mine," Tobe McLaws, who was only seventeen himself, said as he bared his back.

Tobe's cousin Bucky Fletcher, also in our mess, was hands-down winner of the lice prize. He was inhabited by a small army of the vermin.

"I'll be findin' us a cake of good lye," the lieutenant announced. "Tomorrow we clip hair and have a proper scrub."

"Best we take you along with us, Red Cap," Tobe said. "Drown yer graybacks, too."

"And scrub his clothes," Lewis added. "They got a powerful scent."

"Ain't just the clothes," Bucky said, and I laughed along with them.

Next day, once I'd beat the morning calls and Lewis had taken his turn at guard, we marched north beyond the train tracks to where the stream deepened. We plunged into the water like madmen, splashing around and tearing off our clothes.

I hadn't had a real bath in I don't know how long, and even then I hadn't had soap. The harsh lye and a coarse brush tore pounds of grit and infestation from me. Lieutenant Jones produced some shears, and he hacked away at my mane so I felt near bald. What remained got lathered up proper, and the lice began beating a retreat.

"Feel almost lonesome fer the critters," Bucky said as he pointed to the mounds of sludge hugging the far bank.

"Not me," I declared. "They've eaten enough of me."

"That's a truth," Lewis said, frowning at the pitiful creature I had become. "You make a terrible testament to war, naked and all, Red Cap."

"You don't seem so much yourself, Lewis Jones," I barked. As he turned, I saw the neat red scars left by Union bullets, and I froze.

"Nearly got me with that 'un," he said, following my eyes down his side. "Yanks took a powerful dislike to me at Sharpsburg. Shot me twice. Once at Second Manassas. That was just a nick, though. Look to Johnny's head there. Just about planted him."

The lieutenant revealed an ugly slice missing from his left temple. I sighed and shivered.

"Don't let it worry you none, Red Cap," Tobe said, slapping me on the back. "We don't hold it against you boys. Just glad you don't shoot straighter."

They had a good hoot and splashed around some. I scrubbed my rags and rinsed off the soap. Then I stumbled ashore and stretched out under the warming rays of the March sun.

We dried our clothes in the branches of nearby trees. Afterward, as we dressed, I felt their eyes resting on me. Only the little coat I'd gotten in Richmond was still in one piece. My knee trousers were perfectly shredded, and the underthings were past salvaging.

"Here," Lewis said, wrapping his shirt around my waist. "Can't have our drummer outragin' the local womenfolk."

When we got back to camp, he saw me into his tent before retrieving his shirt and heading off.

"Lewis?" I called.

"Gone to fetch you a surprise," Tobe announced with a chuckle.

Surprise was right. Lewis reappeared with a pair of good denim britches, some white cotton drawers, a blue shirt with two rows of shiny brass buttons, and a pair of boots with hardly a trace of wear.

"Where?" I gasped. "How . . ."

"Belonged to little Edgar Fitch," Lewis explained. "Our drummer gone to glory. We were going to send these to his ma, but I guess you need 'em more."

"Edgar wouldn't begrudge you," Buck added. "You treat that drum o' his near as dear as he did. He'd offer the boots himself, I believe, to anybody what loved that drum."

As I exchanged my tattered clothes for the reb drummer's things, I searched the eyes of my companions. Warmth seemed to flow from those faces. They had adopted me. I was their friend.

Later, as I beat retreat, I gazed around me at that regiment of ragged and ill-fed Alabamans. They weren't many of them ten years my senior. Just boys themselves, really. To call them an army was a mighty big stretch.

Their own needs were great, and yet they shared what they had with generous hearts. I wouldn't sign any parole, but I made a secret vow then and there. I wouldn't bring them harm. And as for Lewis, he was the big brother I'd never had.

10

My days with the Alabama boys started early and ended late. The Confederate army had as many calls as our own, and you could keep busy drumming. Whenever their colonel was off recruiting, though, as he was most of the time, camp life settled down considerably. The full regiment had guard duty, but as it happened, every man stood two four-hour stretches on the stockade or in the little forts outside each day. The rest of the day was his own.

Lewis's brother, Lieutenant Johnny, worked things so I always had somebody around to look after me. At first I thought the lieutenant figured I required watching. I saw later he fretted I'd get lonely or else fall into bad habits with some of the younger rebs. John W. Jones was a certified Baptist and looked with disfavor on gambling and drinking. So it was that most days, after beating assembly, I'd find myself in what wasn't altogether the worst kind of sur-roundings.

Sometimes I'd follow Tobe and Buck down to the creek for a swim. Later they'd dip lines in the water and snag a catfish or a perch. Once in a while I'd try my luck, but I didn't have the knack. They asked me along, though, on condition I'd dig a few worms and help clean the fish.

Whenever Lewis was relieved from guard duty, we'd set off for the woods. We'd walk together, sharing tales of our battles and our homes. I told of Enos and Ollie, and he spoke of the day at Antietam Creek when three-fourths of his company were shot down.

Mostly, though, he taught me about the plants and the animals. He'd take his musket along, and when we spied a squirrel or a rabbit, there was certain to be meat for the supper pot.

"Never knew any man with such a shooter's eye," I declared.

"People take to shootin' at you, it improves your aim," he explained. "And we never have many balls put by. We got to hit the mark first try or run for cover!"

One day around the middle of March he found deer tracks. We crept along quietly for half a mile or so before Lewis discovered three animals chewing grass beside a small pond. He rammed a ball down his musket barrel and took aim. Then, smiling, he swung the gun over so I could have a try. I shook my head and declined. After all, I'd only been hunting a few times with Pa, and then I'd used a fowling piece. Those clumsy reb muskets were near as heavy as I was.

Lewis helped me balance the musket, though, and amazingly the deer stayed where they were. I aimed, took a deep breath, and fired. A world of smoke stung my face and burned my eyes. When it cleared, I saw two deer rushing past the pond into the trees beyond. The third lay bleeding out its life before us.

"You got a fair eye yourself, Red Cap," he said.

"That's not my name, you know," I told him. "It's Ransom. Back with the Tenth they called me R. J., but at home my friends know me as Ranse."

"Then that's what I'll use," he said, taking the musket and leading the way toward the deer.

"Seems to me you took a mighty big chance, giving me your gun, Lewis."

"How's that?"

"I could've shot you, or maybe run off."

"I figure you've had opportunities aplenty to do that," he said, scratching his chin. "Sometimes I ponder why you stay. You got good folks waitin' for you back home, and you could pass for a Virginian easy. Bet you could find your way north. Young as you are, and pretty to look at, folks'd help you."

"Pretty?"

"Once yer hair grows back, you'll be pretty as a girl. Not meanin' that as a mark against you, Ranse," he said when I frowned. "Just sayin' ladies'd find it easy to help you."

"It's how I got my coat," I told him. "If I was toad ugly, would you boys have taken me in?"

"Wasn't yer face touched my heart," Lewis said, setting the rifle aside and drawing his knife. "Was yer size. Seein' you a prisoner of war aroused the tender feelings of my heart. The way you looked me dead center in the eye and announced you had nothin' left to rob! Why, I thought you a midget general. Colonel at least. I got to talking to Johnny thereafter. Ain't either of us'll abide the notion of makin' war on children. You ain't seen the army of little 'uns up in Virginia made orphans by this fool fightin'. We had some youngsters no older'n you march into Maryland with us.

95

Left 'em behind in a Sharpsburg cornfield. I knowed hard times as a boy myself. Wouldn't wish it on a soul."

"You're ancient now, after all," I said, laughing.

"Wasn't but twenty when this fuss started. Must be eighty or ninety now. Seein' what I seen ages a man past reckonin'."

Ages a boy, too, I thought.

We cooked up venison steaks that night for Lewis's whole company. Afterward we sang for their colonel.

"Lewis, there's a fair portion of meat left," I observed as we took to our blankets that night.

"Last us a day or so at least," he noted.

"I was wondering if I might not have a bit of it to take to my friends inside the stockade. They're starving, you know, and a couple of them are sick."

"I got the guard, but Tobe and Buck can take you. Eh, boys?"

The two younger Alabamans readily agreed, and it was settled. We managed to take a few onions along, too, plus a sack of beans.

"Glory be!" Red shouted when I arrived. "Poland! Fetch the others. We got company!"

They were glad to see me even before I presented my gift. Thereafter they were close to religious with their praise.

"You ain't forgot your messmates after all," Poland cried.

"Finally got some boots, too," Jimmy Dyer observed. "You rebs treat Red Cap right. Elsewise we'll have to storm the stockade and chastise you proper."

"Wouldn't worry about R. J.," Red said, chewing an onion. "It's them rebs likely to be in peril."

I shook hands and exchanged news. Then Tobe announced a sergeant coming, and we said our good-byes.

"I'll bring more when I can," I promised.

"You do that," Poland said. "Watch out for raiders, though. The rascals get more darin' every day."

I noticed bruises on Poland's arms and forehead. I read the hunger in Sam's eyes, the despair and disease plaguing others. I cried inside for their plight, and I felt guilty for the good fortune that had come my way.

As we left the stockade I watched the envious eyes of the other prisoners. Their looks haunted me. And that night I tossed and turned in my blankets, tormented by all sorts of imagined cruelties.

Then a yellow-haired spectre appeared in my dream.

"So, Ranny, are you thinkin' you should ask to go back to the stockade?" a familiar voice asked. I stared hard at the phantom, not wanting to believe in it. But it refused to leave. I was staring at Danny's ghost.

"You're dead," I scolded. "Ought to let the living rest."

"I do that and I'm sure to have company out here. You fool, it ain't all that pleasant bein' dead. Wait a spell. And what about Red and the rest? That extra food'll get them through lean days."

"I miss you, Danny," I whimpered.

"Well, I guess so. You ain't done any good pranks since I left. Don't you go actin' all guilty now. Only reason it was me shot and not you is the Lord figured He'd leave the one down there who was less addled. Don't go changin' His mind."

"Danny?" I called as the vision faded. "Danny!"

Lewis shook me awake.

"Lord, Ranse, you had yourself a nightmare," Tobe said when I blinked the dream from my eyes.

"Was the stockade," Lewis judged. "I look down from my

roost and wonder how anybody lives more'n a few days there."

"Nobody lives there at all," I argued. "They survive, maybe, but can't anybody really live in that place."

It got no better when the stockade was completed on March 23. The weather warmed, and there was scant breeze now to offer respite. Two days later Camp Sumter got itself a new commander, a German-speaking fellow named Wirz. Next thing I knew he was making all sorts of changes.

"It's a crime," Lewis told me. "Each mornin' we have a standin' roll call. Takes two or three hours now the compound's fillin' up. Men go to droppin' right and left."

To top that, Wirz ordered the simple hundred man ration companies discarded. New groups of ninety were counted off. When the men argued over that foolishness, the little captain had himself a regular screaming fit.

"Cussed and kicked like thunder, I tell you," Tobe said, shaking his head. "Warned he'd tolerate no rebellion, and he's stopped rations."

I saw for myself after beating guard mount. Lieutenant Jones took me along with him to the gate, and I saw the men staring helplessly at us, praying the ration wagon would appear. For two days this went on.

"Guess he aims to starve 'em into behavin'," the lieutenant muttered. "Won't work."

Wirz satisfied himself it had, though, for he resumed issuing rations the third day. He didn't make good the lost food, though, and the starving took its toll. Was right afterward Sam Brooks died.

I beat taps for Sam and cried inside. I knew he wouldn't be the last.

Rumors of exchange never entirely left Andersonville, but some preachers visited us in April and spoke of a sort of general exchange of all prisoners planned for Easter. It didn't happen, but it sure was talked about.

Some changes did come, though. The stockade continued to fill up with prisoners as trainload after trainload arrived. Rations inside and outside the stockade dwindled, and new diseases spread their fury. Captain Wirz complained he needed more guards and that the two regiments he had ought to spend more time on his walls.

"Yu 'Bamans ees lazy," he shouted one morning in early May.

"Pretty soon he'll have cause to remember us fondly," Lieutenant Jones told Lewis. I looked at him nervously, and Lewis gripped my shoulders.

"Meant to talk to you 'bout this, Ranse," Lewis said, leading me to his tent. "Be headed back to the fightin' fore long."

I grew pale, and my legs went numb.

"It was bound to happen," Lewis explained. "We're a veteran regiment, and any batch of old men and schoolboys can sit atop a wall and guard prisoners."

"Sure," I mumbled. "Rob and shoot us. Starve us. We had a corporal in Richmond swore he'd killed more Yanks from cutting rations than a whole brigade could drop on the battlefield."

"There's truth to that," Lewis admitted, "but they got armies up in Tennessee ready to march south. I joined in the first place to defend my home. I aim to do it."

"Still got the heart for killing Yanks, do you?"

"Never did," he said, scowling. "Less so after knowin' you, son."

The lieutenant joined us then. Lewis nodded, and the officer sat down on his blankets.

"Why'd you muster into this war, Ranse?" he asked.

"Partly to put an end to slavery," I replied. "Partly to have an adventure. My friends were all off to fight, and I hated being left behind."

"And if you were decidin' today?" Lewis asked.

"I'm not. I don't know what I'd do," I confessed. "It's been hard on me mostly. I've been hungry and cold. I've had more than a few cross words sent my way, and there've been men to make fun of me being small. Still, I've known good friends, and I've learned a few things. One day, if I live to tell about them, there'll be some fine tales to spin."

"You know there's more'n a few Marylanders wearin' the gray," Lewis pointed out. "We're still in powerful need of a drummer."

"I couldn't!" I barked.

"I know 'bout your pledge, Ranse, but you was hardly old enough to know what you was doin'," the lieutenant asserted. "Any other reason for you to stick by the blue?"

"I never held with slavery."

"We look like planters?" Lewis asked. "Ain't about that."

"What then?"

"It's about bein' left alone, givin' a man the right to choose things for himself."

"Did you see those men that built the stockade?" I cried. "They look to be choosing?"

"Let's not take to arguin', not with such little time left," Lieutenant Jones said, swallowing hard. "Ain't Lewis or me, neither, apt to sleep knowin' you got put back in that stockade."

"I'd put you on a northbound train myself 'fore that," Lewis added.

"You got some education, Ranse," his brother observed. "Read just fine? Write a good hand?"

"My teacher back in Frostburg said it was the best in town."

"I spoke with Cap'n Wirz," the lieutenant went on to say. "He's in need of an orderly. Wants somebody he can trust, who'll follow orders, and who can keep accounts. Up to the task?"

"Would I have to sign a parole?" I asked.

"You couldn't run off," Lewis said. "And there'll be some who'd look upon the work as aidin' your enemies."

"Wirz'd see you were proper fed, though," the lieutenant argued. "And he's got some other boys workin' in his office. You'd have friends."

"When will you leave?"

"Before the week's out," Lieutenant Jones answered.

"I got to answer now then."

"It's an easy choice, son," Lewis told me. "Livin' with Wirz or dyin' in that stockade."

Something in his eyes told me it was the truth. And I suppose a man's bound to choose life over death. I told them I would work for Wirz.

That next day Lewis and I went on a final hunt. I shot a rabbit, and he bagged three. We cooked them on spits, and I took mine to my friends inside the stockade. Tobe and Bucky escorted me.

"You're a welcome sight," Red Armhult told me when I handed over the rabbit. "Sit down a moment."

"Just got a minute or so," I explained. "Have to hurry

back and help the Alabamans pack up. They go north tomorrow."

"Heard," Red said, frowning. "They started puttin' them Georgia reserve boys atop the roosts this evenin', them and their old Queen Anne muskets. You stay clear o' that deadline, R. J."

"I will," I promised. "I have a couple of escorts. Where's everybody got to?"

"Jimmy and Poland went down by the hospital to fetch Georgie Blackburn."

"Oh?" I asked, reading the sadness in his eyes. "He sick?"

"Won't George ever be sick again, R. J. Went and died, ole George did."

I frowned. I'd never been close to Blackburn. Still, he was one of the Tenth. "I should've gotten some fruit for him."

"You did more'n was possible already, R. J.," Red told me. "We gave him every carrot, even two onions put by. He gave up, boy. Dyin' ain't long in comin' when you do that."

First Sam. Now Blackburn. "I'll miss them," I said, setting down the rabbit and rubbing my eyes.

"He asked somethin' of you, R. J."

"Anything," I answered without hesitation.

"Wanted you to beat the drum when they put him under. Like you done for Sam."

"I'll sure do it."

"First thing tomorrow they'll do the buryin'. They sendin' you back to us when they leave, them Alabamans?"

"Found me a job with Wirz."

"Wirz? He's a mean one, R. J."

"Do my best to stay out where I can come by help for you. Inside, I'd just shorten your rations."

"Be good company, though," Red said. "Still, I wouldn't wish a friend into this place."

"Nor an enemy, even," I added.

On the morning of May 9, I played taps as a weary Johnny Poland helped Red place George Blackburn in a trench cut in the red Georgia clay. Three days later I beat assembly for the Twenty-sixth Alabama. The proud regiment then packed up its baggage and loaded it onto a train. Before leaving, though, they marched past the gates of the stockade. In a rare show of respect, the Alabamans presented arms as they passed. Thousands of Yankee wretches raised a cheer for their departing guards.

"Hurrah for Alabama!" howled one mess.

"Shoot ole Grant!" somebody urged. "George Meade wouldn't argue against an exchange."

I gazed at Company I and fought to keep my legs from weakening. As Lewis appeared, I raised my arm in a stiff salute. He winked, and Tobe waved me over.

"Watch yer hide, Red Cap," somebody called.

"Yeah, boy, we'll miss yer drummin'."

Me, I'd miss it, too. Drums were hard to come by, and the one I'd inherited was aboard the train awaiting fresh hands.

"March with us a bit, Ranse," Lewis urged, and I found myself accompanying them to the station. I stood on the platform as the Twenty-sixth boarded the train. I was still there when the last car vanished from view, headed north.

"Come along now, boy," a white-haired old rebel finally said, waving me along. "Cap Wirz'll be wantin' you."

"Yes, sir," I said, marching stiffly at his side. And all the while we walked I wondered if I wasn't embarking on a whole new nightmare.

11

I met Captain Wirz half an hour later at the little room for orderlies that led to his office. He was an undersized, fidgety fellow, with a jaw that stuck forward and a pointed, ratlike nose. His small eyes blazed with intensity, and he was forever throwing his hands behind him and pacing back and forth.

He wasn't the sort of man you'd take for an officer. He wore plain gray trousers and a calico shirt, and the only hint of a soldier was the worn gray kepi whose bill had the odd habit of dropping down over his forehead. He stuffed an odd-looking pistol in his belt, and I was staring at the strange gun's many barrels when he turned his attention to me.

"Yu writes gut, does yu?" he asked, examining my fingers as if that would attest to the fact.

"Yes, sir," I answered.

"Got much verk for yu. Hard verk. Yu can do?"

"Yes, sir," I promised. "I've been used to hard work all my life."

"Vell, ve see 'bout dat," he grumbled. "Yu verk gut, ve treat yu gut. Yu do as I say, ja? Ja, Red Cap?"

"Yes, sir," I responded again.

"Den ve get along."

With that said, he marched out the door and headed for the stockade. Once he was clear of the place, three boys outfitted in fine blue wool stepped inside.

"I'm Jim Stevens," the tallest of the lot, a walnut-haired boy with sky-blue eyes, said, offering his hand. "This here," he added, shoving forward a shorter yellow-haired boy, "is Cable Jackson. The runt there's Matthew Bailey."

The smallest gave me a nod. Even he was half a head taller than I was.

"R. J. Powell," I announced as I shook hands with each of them in turn. "Tenth West Virginia Infantry."

"Drummer?" Cable asked.

I nodded, noticing their caps had bright brass bugles on them.

"I've been envying you some, seeing you off at the creek with those Alabamans," Jim told me. "We don't have many chances to swim."

"Be better now there's four," Cable said.

" 'Cept there's more prisoners coming," Jim argued. "And R. J. here's supposed to help with the accounts. The rest of us just tend to errands for the captain."

"Been here long?" I asked.

"Few weeks," Jim explained. "Matthew and I drummed for the Eighty-fifth New York. Cable there's from the 103d Pennsylvania."

"Where's home?" I asked Cable.

"York," he told me. " 'Less the rebs burned it when they were up to Gettysburg."

"I'm from Frostburg, in Maryland," I explained.

"Been there," Cable said. "I used to work some for my uncle. He was a freighter. When he joined up, so did I."

"Jim and I come right out of the Orphans' Home," Matthew boasted, spitting out the door. "Didn't think it could be worse in the army, but it's been trying."

"Has at that," I agreed. "Where'd you come by the uniforms? They look fresh cut."

"Our colonel had mine tailored in Harrisburg," Cable explained.

"Got ours from a reb needle man," Jim added. "Plenty of blue cloth down here, you know. Not much in demand. That was in Plymouth, North Carolina. Was there we was took captive."

"We're Plymouth pilgrims," Matthew said, grinning. "At least that's what folks call us. The whole bunch of us, better part of a brigade, got trapped there when a reb ram, the *Albemarle*, drove off our supply ships."

"And you kept your clothes?" I asked.

"Fell in with honest rebs," Cable said, laughing. "Hard to come by, I hear. It's been tough on the fellows in the stockade. Too long a time on garrison duty. All of us been town raised, and my company's already had three dead."

"His uncle," Jim explained. "Cracked over the head by one of Mosby's boys. Seems the bugs and bad food aren't killing us fast enough."

"Uncle Jack had three hundred dollars on him," Cable said sourly. "They beat him, robbed him, even took his clothes. I didn't know he was dead till he was in the ground three whole days."

"You've been here right along?" I asked.

"Some Alabama fellow culled us from the trainload," Jim

said. "Spared us the worst. We even kept our money. Got dollars to swap in town for food."

"A Yankee dollar buys a bushel of carrots," Cable boasted.

"Don't the rebs feed you?" I asked.

"Double rations, but the food's still poor," Jim grumbled. "Once I'm a bit bigger, I'll go up to Macon and work in a sawmill. They pay you for that sort of work."

"I'm not working for any rebs!" Cable vowed. "Rather be tossed into the stockade."

"You keep up your bad habits, you will be," Jim said.

Cable laughed. After glancing out the door to make sure no one was approaching, he slipped his suspenders past his shoulders and exposed his rump. A fair crisscross pattern of red stripes painted the white flesh.

"You been caned!" I cried.

"I tipped an inkwell," Cable explained, "and spilled ink."

"It's not so bad here, R. J.," Jim declared. "Just keep clear of the captain's temper. He's got a hair trigger for meanness, and all of us know it."

"He hits hard," Cable added. "No worse than my own sergeant would give me, though."

The sight of those stripes unsettled me, and I knew I wasn't sharing Lewis's tent anymore. Nor was I under Red's watchful eye. I was purely on my own.

Captain Wirz found plenty of work for me. He was Swiss and claimed a doctor's training, but his hand was a wild scrawl, and he wasn't well acquainted with English. He couldn't say a dozen words without throwing out a curse. Sometimes I didn't even figure out what he'd said till later.

The little captain made few friends inside the stockade. Now that might have seemed only natural, him being a jailer after all. But those Alabama boys had earned our respect by treating us decent, and looking at us eye to eye. Captain Wirz, who was badly wounded near Richmond, had a near useless right hand. It hurt bad, and often he stared at prisoners with pure grain hatred.

One day, when I accompanied him inside the stockade, a band of Pennsylvanians asked if something could be done about the cornmeal they were given.

"Ees gut enuff for Yankees!" Wirz screamed. "Ja, I can do someding. I can stop rations!"

The Penn boys quickly abandoned their complaint.

"It's his favorite trick," Red told me when I paid him a call. "That devil has two- to three-hour roll calls every day, you know. We lose three or four men from it each time. We're issued rations for three groups of ninety each—same as what we got for a hundred. It's too little food for too many men, I tell you, R. J."

Wirz's favorite pastime was looking for tunnels. Quite a few were dug, mostly using wells as a start. More than one brave soldier lost his life when the walls collapsed on him. Others were run down by hounds and chewed to pieces. Many escape attempts were foiled by some N'Yawker.

Life inside the stockade was growing more perilous by the day. Forty or fifty dead were carried to the gate to await burial every morning. Once in a while Cable got permission to beat his drum for some comrade. He'd managed to keep that drum in spite of everything, and he guarded it like a mama bear protects her cubs.

"Now that Uncle Jack's gone, it's all I have," he told me one night as we huddled in the orderly room. Jim and Matthew were already fast asleep, but a sudden cold had struck Georgia, and my quilt was unable to fend off the frigid torment. "Sometimes when the cap's gone I beat out a march or two, and we sing. I expect you did the same with those Alabamans. Miss it?"

"I miss the music," I confessed. "But mostly I miss the laughing. Those rebs knew how to bring on a smile. And they always had fresh meat around."

"Maybe we'll go fishing next time the cap sends us to town."

"Be welcome, Cable."

Any break from the long, tedious hours I spent hunched over Wirz's account books was welcome. And when I had them current, the captain brought orders to be copied or letters to be written. He was always complaining to Richmond about the lack of guards, the slow flow of supplies, and the inadequate medical corps.

One complaint, about an outbreak of smallpox, did bring results. A doc arrived and gave vaccinations to the most likely sufferers. The vaccine had a terrifying effect, though. The scars festered and ate away at arms. In the end most of the poor men died, and those who lived lost arms.

"Another reb plot to murder good soldiers," Red judged. I heard from Cable the reb docs were beside themselves—thunderstruck. It seemed that scurvy turned the vaccine into a killer. And there wasn't a man long in Andersonville not acquainted with scurvy.

I was leaning over my ledgers the day we had our first delegation from town visit the captain. Mainly they were ladies. They claimed to be grieved at stories of the suffering inside the stockade and wanted to visit the place. Captain Wirz arranged a brief tour. Three of the women, I heard, fainted before they got to the gate. Was the smell, Cable said. Anyhow, some of the visiting ladies returned, bringing such food as could be spared and offering blankets and clothes.

110

I believe the reb guards wound up with most of it, though I don't know for certain. I did hear the captain denouncing General Grant for being responsible for great suffering on both sides.

"Dat devil Grant's de blame!" he screamed.

Nevertheless Wirz sent his four orderlies into town with a thank-you message. We were led to a modest house near the church and treated to a genuine feast of baked ham, sweet potatoes, peas, carrots, and peach pie.

"You youngsters are orphans, I understand," a Mrs. Pratt Winslow said. "I've lost my own boys to childhood fever, and a daughter to a fall from a horse. I wonder if any of you'd consider coming to live with me as my adopted son? Mrs. Ames here is of like mind, and I'm certain we can find homes for all of you."

"I have family," I announced. I didn't add I had no more intention of becoming some reb lady's pet than mustering into Confederate service.

"Oh, and it was you I had my heart set on, youngster," Mrs. Winslow cried in disappointment. "Perhaps this other small one would choose otherwise," she said, turning to Matthew.

"We'd have peach pie?" Matthew asked. "And time to go fishing?"

"School as well. And a pony of your own."

"Jim could come, too?" Matthew asked, nudging his taller friend.

"I'd be delighted if Jim would share my home," Mrs. Ames announced. "I've lost my husband, and it's only me and my twins. They're seven, you see, and certain to need a brother's guiding hand."

"I'm bound to learn a carpenter's trade," Jim told her.

"I believe you could do even better," Mrs. Ames argued. "I have land, you see, and a cotton gin. A stable of horses. In time you would manage the property, of course."

The two New York boys smiled.

"Now, as to you, young man," Mrs. Winslow said, speaking to Cable, "there are ladies waiting on the veranda with an eye to adopt. If you'll follow me, I'll take you out to see them."

Cable started to object, but two tall gentlemen lifted him from his chair and bore him along. I stared in disbelief as they showed him like a prize colt.

"I ain't a slave come to auction!" Cable growled finally, and the people backed away. "I'm a prisoner of war. We've all of us got duties at the camp. Captain Wirz—"

"Oh, the captain has already agreed to let us have you," Mrs. Winslow explained. "We're to furnish laborers for the fortifications."

I grew pale. We were goods to be bartered.

"Let's go," I urged my companions. "Cable's right. We're not slaves to be auctioned."

"Speak for yourself," Jim said, shoving me away. "You never been an orphan. What's the army ever brought me except cold and hunger? Did you hear that woman? I'm to manage a farm."

"We'll have pie to eat," Matthew added. "And be rid of that captain's cane."

"Cable?" I asked, turning to him.

"Leave them to their choice," he suggested. "Let's go."

We trudged past the disappointed southerners and made our way past Anderson Station to the camp. We didn't return to the orderly room straight away. Instead we headed off into the pines and walked to the creek.

I hadn't had a swim in two weeks, and I slipped out of my clothes and stepped into the cool water. Cable joined me, and we splashed and swam and laughed like a pair of loons. By and by a band of boys off guard duty came along and hopped in as well. Taller by a bit and hide-toughened from rough duty, those Georgia reserves proved as water-crazed as Cable and me. We were all of us just boys for a while. Shy of our uniforms, you couldn't tell Yank from reb, and there weren't many of the Georgians much past fourteen or fifteen. Wasn't a hint of whiskers to the bunch, and we appeared to all the world to be a gang of country boys sharing the first trace of summer.

We weren't, though. Andersonville had added invisible years.

"Can't really blame Jim and Matthew," Cable told me later when we dressed. "It's a powerful urge, to have family."

"You got anybody?" I asked.

"Not since Uncle Jack died. But I won't forget my duty in return for a pony or some peach pie. I'm a soldier, even if I'm just fourteen."

I nodded my agreement, and we marched in step back to the orderly room.

With just the two of us, our labors doubled. Captain Wirz did find a few boys to run his errands, but they never lasted long. They'd turn sick or else not take to the work.

"Ees gut I have two gut boys," he boasted. "I never get my verk done."

"Maybe we shouldn't be doing this," I told Cable. "Aren't we helping the enemy?"

"Somebody'd do it," he argued. "And besides, I smuggle in food to my company."

I stared at him in disbelief.

113

"Me, too," I confessed.

"But that's nothing," he added, drawing out a sheet of paper from his pocket. "Look at this. It's an escape map. I copy it every chance I get and take the copies inside."

"Lot of good it would do," I grumbled. "Those that run always get caught."

"Not all," he said, laughing to himself. "Five so far've made it using my maps. I get them to a plantation on Flint River. There are slaves there who help them along to Tennessee. So you see I figure to be still fighting this war."

"Lord, Cable, if you get caught . . ."

"They can't do much more than shoot me," he declared. "That's always been a soldier's risk, hasn't it?"

And so I embarked on a new career. I became Cable's eager accomplice. Not only did we smuggle food, but we supplied maps. Later on we got hold of a schedule of arriving prisoners, and thereafter we let the men inside know when they might grab a boxcar bound for Macon.

"R. J., watch you don't get caught in this commerce," Red warned me when I delivered my first batch of maps. "There's a hundred men in this place ready to sell your hide to old Wirz. And as for escape, there isn't a Company I man left with the strength to try it."

Nevertheless three Massachusetts boys made a try in the middle of June. One was shot by a Georgia reserve boy not as tall as his musket. A second was treed by a hound. The third got halfway to Macon before a farmer shot him for looting his corn crib.

"At least he had his run," Cable said sadly. "Better than waiting for the fevers to take you."

12

Andersonville contained over twelve thousand men in May. That didn't count the thousand who had died. By mid-June there were twenty-two thousand—and another two hundred had died. It went on and on that way. Rations grew scanter for everyone—guards included. If not for the kind gifts of townspeople, I would have wasted away to nothing. Cable and I never returned without a few peaches or a bag of potatoes.

I never understood how, with thousands starving inside the stockade, the rebs never managed to buy vegetables off the local farmers or send parties into the woods for game. The Georgia reserves managed it easy enough. By late June a pair of onions sold inside for five Yankee dollars. I don't think there was a soul in Company I with a button left. Those young Georgia guards had a particular fondness for uniform buttons emblazoned with the Union eagle.

I smuggled what I could inside the stockade when I accompanied Captain Wirz on his tunnel-hunting trips. Other times I visited my old comrades, bringing grim news of the terrible fighting in the Wilderness and at Spotsylvania, up in Virginia.

"Means even more boys coming to Andersonville," Red observed.

Lately he'd grown gaunt, and he was barely able to stand for roll call. Johnny Poland said it was the diarrhea. More than that, though, Red was giving up. I could see him gazing off past the wall and talking of home. The heat and the insects and the suffocating stench were taking their toll.

On June 23 Billy Stagg joined the dead. Next day C. D. Porrellson, another Company I private, passed on. It seemed the company was thinning out daily. Then Cable brought word from Poland I should find an excuse to visit the stockade.

"Somebody else's died," I muttered.

"Some poor fellow's dying every hour nowadays," Cable said, nodding. "All my old friends from York are gone."

The Plymouth pilgrims were hard hit, all right, but so were the old-timers, as we who'd come to Andersonville in February and March were known. It wasn't that we were soft, like the pilgrims. We'd known hardship aplenty. But six, seven months of prison life was too much for us. Even the oldest was young by anyone's reckoning, and a young man needs sun and sky and air and space.

I slipped inside the stockade with the ration wagon and found my way to the tattered remnant of our old shebang. Poland took me inside, and I knelt beside Red. He was wasted to skin and bone, and his eyes were already dead. He could barely squeeze my fingers, this man who not so long ago had easily carried me on one shoulder.

"R. J., I'd have you write a letter to my family," he

116

whispered. "Don't tell 'em how I went. It'd pain 'em some. Speak of our high times together in the Shenandoah Valley."

"I will," I promised.

"One thing more," he said, growing somber. "I'd have you sing for me. A hymn maybe. We had a little quartet yonder past the Illinois boys, but two of 'em died off. Then, too, maybe you could drum me taps when they cover me up."

"You'll get well," I argued.

"Don't go lyin' now, son. Ain't any of us foolin' ourselves on that account. Didn't figure to outlast that rascal Stagg. I am surprised Jimmy Dyer ain't died, though. I had ten pounds on him through May."

I nodded, and Jimmy crept over and announced he was better acquainted with prayers.

"It's you who kept us together, Corporal," Jimmy added. "Don't know what we'll do now."

"Follow Poland's lead," Red advised. "He's atoned for leavin' us last year. Bet you wish you'd stayed home, don't you, Johnny?"

"And miss R. J.'s singin'?" Poland asked. "And all this fine reb food?"

We laughed a moment. Then I sang. After two hymns the tears welled up in my eyes, and I couldn't continue. Red smiled faintly as I clasped his hand. Then Cable arrived with word the captain was asking after me.

"Best come, R. J.," Cable urged. "Cap's already kicked the desk twice."

"Go," Poland said. "We'll tend to what's needed."

I followed Cable back to the orderly room. Captain Wirz had a regular fit when he saw me.

"Red Cap, yu ees lazy!" he screamed. "Look at all dees paper I got to send Richmond. Copy dem. Now!"

I hurried past him to the desk, receiving a sharp poke in the ribs from his fingers. He cussed me roundly before setting off to tend some other worry.

"Cable, I thank you," I said after the captain had left.

"Wasn't any trouble. We're messmates, after all."

"Then maybe you'd do me a bigger favor?" I asked.

"What'd that be?"

"I got a man who's dying in my company. A corporal who saved my hide a dozen times, and he's asked me to beat taps for him."

"You're welcome to my drum," he told me. "And if you don't figure I'd be an intruder, I'd go along with you."

"You'd be welcome, Cabe."

So he was. When word came Red had passed, I followed the men carrying the dead to the graveyard. Staring at the near-naked skeleton that had once been Red Armhult, I could hardly keep my balance. I drummed long and loud, better than I'd ever done before. And I prayed God would find Red a soft, warm meadow to rest in.

Jimmy Dyer outlasted Red twelve days. Besides Johnny Poland and myself, there were only three Company I boys left alive in Andersonville.

As expected, the battles around Richmond had brought new trains of prisoners to Andersonville. General William T. Sherman and his western army were moving on Atlanta, too. There were nearly thirty thousand on hand now, and it was hard to find a path to walk to the sinks. Midsummer heat turned the stream into a boiling mass of maggots. The odor kept all but the most determined away.

On July 3, three hundred and fifty West Virginians arrived. I recognized some from my valley campaigning, and we waved at one another as they marched past on their way

118

to the gate. Like the Plymouth prisoners, they hadn't yet been robbed, and there were so many of them the Georgia reserves didn't do a thorough job, either. They got inside the stockade with good boots, overcoats, and even watches and greenbacks.

I heard the first scream myself. Mosby's raiders wasted not a minute in falling on the newcomers. Being mountain folk mainly, they resisted considerably, but the raiders were ruthless. Wasn't any time at all, though, before cries for help rose louder and louder. The whole prison seemed to be alive with pleas. Even the Georgia reserves joined in. A couple of raiders thrown back toward the deadline were cut down by reb marksmen, giving the brutalized West Virginians new heart.

"Give us a stick and we'll beat 'em silly!" somebody shouted.

Captain Wirz muttered about Yankee vermin, thieves, and cutthroats. Then, wonder of wonders, he ordered clubs handed into the prison. Cable and I raced to the gate to get a look at the melee.

"Yu vant dees raiders, ja?" the captain asked. "Yu get dem den."

Instantly the small party of regulators, as the men pledged to justice and fair play called themselves, drove a wedge between the raiders and their victims. Soon it was the raiders on the defensive. Murderers, thieves, and villains, the lot of them! And now they were driven to cover. Some were forced across the deadline.

"Don't shoot, little reb!" one man screamed as he tossed silver coins toward the guard's roost. The young Georgian took aim with his antiquated Queen Anne musket and parted the raider's hair.

Other raiders were driven into the filth beside the stream. Two men sank in the muck—were just swallowed whole.

One by one the raiders were beaten silly or else subdued and tied. The next day, July 4, Independence Day, was celebrated by a parade of the shackled raiders, including Captain Mosby himself. Then, on the fifth, the regulators held a trial.

There was a jury, counsel, the whole works. Poland told me it was fair, for most got off with some time in stocks, or strung up by the thumbs. Six were picked to hang. Wirz supplied lumber, and a scaffold was built.

Cable and I weren't the only ones to smuggle ourselves inside for a view of the executions. It was something to see those six. Big, healthy, strong as oxen, their health attested to high crimes so far as I was concerned. They were roundly hooted. Ole Mosby, whose real name was Collins, complained he'd never hurt anybody and was only moved by circumstance to evil deeds.

Nobody who remembered his cruelties, at Andersonville and before that at Belle Isle, had much patience for such a speech.

The entertainment came when one of the men broke loose and tried to escape. He led his pursuers on a merry chase, but he couldn't get past the swamp down by the sinks, and he was dragged back to the scaffold. When a raider named Sarsfield began to argue like a lawyer, the crowd decided it had waited long enough.

"Don't lay it on so thick, you villain!" one soldier yelled.

"Cut it short," another urged.

"Less talkin' and more hangin'!" three or four suggested.

At eleven o'clock that morning the raiders were blindfolded. Their hands and feet were bound, and they were led out onto planks once nooses were put into place. The planks were pulled away, and the men dropped quick and sudden. Two of them went easy. Sarsfield and another kicked and howled before they strangled. As for Collins, his rope parted, and he sat up, asking if he was in heaven.

"Nobody's ever mistook this place for heaven!" somebody yelled.

Once he figured out what had happened, Collins claimed it was divine intervention, and he should be freed.

"You're just such a rascal it takes two hangin's to get you proper dead," a tall Indiana regulator insisted.

So they hung Collins over. The second time it took.

In July the rebs finally admitted the compound could no longer hold the swimming mass of humanity imprisoned there, and one wall of the stockade was opened up. A big stretch of new ground was available, and the prisoners wasted no time fighting for a spot. This new ground was dry, not infested by insect life, and allowed a man a hair more space.

Opening up the stockade had Wirz edgy. He doubled the guard, and one day he ordered the cannons to fire blank charges as a warning of what might happen should the prisoners attempt a mass escape.

"Those men can barely walk to the sinks," I told Cable. "How are they going to attack cannons?"

It was about that time we heard rumors of rescue, too. There was lots of talk in town of a cavalry raid launched by General Stoneman, commanding Sherman's horse soldiers. It appeared Stoneman's plan was to free the prisoners at Macon and Andersonville so they could help fight Hood at

Atlanta. The general did get to Macon, but not the way he'd planned. He was taken prisoner himself, and seven hundred or so of his men wound up in Andersonville.

Our greatest hope for liberty was still the exchange, and we never entirely lost hope of its resumption. Word of Sherman's march south from Chattanooga was another promising development. But so many of his soldiers— mostly men from the western states—arrived that none of us could really expect an early victory, or liberation, either.

"I hear a hundred died today," Cable told me the first day of August.

"It's possible," I answered.

As we stretched out atop our blankets that night in the sultry confines of the orderly room, I stared out the window at the stars. They seemed clearer than ever in a black sky. Pa once told me whenever I got discouraged to gaze up there and count those stars. You got to thinking about how God put each and every one of them in the sky, and you realized He was sure to have a look down on you.

"I don't know I can believe that after being in this place," Cable said when I shared the tale. "Seems to me old Harry's taking the upper hand hereabouts. The hell the preachers back in York told me about was just sort of practice. The real place is down here in Georgia."

13

August brought the worst heat I ever endured. Even the trees down by the creek began to wilt, and the men inside the stockade withered and died. Tongues swelled up so men couldn't even talk. One man plunged into the mucked remains of Sweetwater Branch—a fine name for that quagmire! He just sank from sight a foot at a time until all that was left was his tattered forage cap. In time it went, too.

Some fellows, starved and parched past endurance, with hair and teeth falling out and joints near sticking through their flesh, stepped over to the deadline and shouted curses at the guards of the Georgia reserves. Pretty soon a Queen Anne musket barked, and a bullet ended some poor wretch's pain.

I saw these things from the north gate or while visiting what was left of Company I. Ladies in town no longer spared food from their empty larders, and if one of them parted with a shirt or a coat, I swapped it to one of the reserves for an orange or peach, an onion or potato. Now, though, when the need inside was greatest, I'd sold every stitch worth a penny. Cable had bought carrots with the last of his greenbacks, too.

"Best you not come inside for a bit," Poland warned. "They say ole Daner's got the typhus, and it's mighty catchin'."

"Sure," I said, dropping my head.

"R. J., don't you go crying over us now. We had a fair run of it here, months longer'n I'd believed possible. Mostly that's been your doin'. You brought what you could. More'n most would've managed."

But not enough, I thought as I left.

I settled in at my desk in the orderly room and copied out Captain Wirz's newest letters. He was again writing everyone he could think of, hoping to improve rations and get replacements for the guards who were dying almost as fast as the prisoners now. Those Georgia boys ran off at an alarming rate, too, most of them weary of Andersonville and homesick to boot. Others worried after their families, especially the ones in the northern part of the state where Sherman was stomping through.

Some of them talked to Cable and me. We never went to town by ourselves now, or visited the stockade alone.

"They aim to share our good fortune," Cable suggested, reminding me of the high times when we could always expect food and friendship from the neighbors.

That didn't explain the escorts inside the stockade, though.

The truth was, Captain Wirz no longer trusted us—me, in particular.

"You got too many friends inside, Red Cap," a freckled Georgia boy named Calvin Peters told me. "I heard Wirz tell the lieutenant to watch you good."

I, of course, should have noticed the change in the captain. He'd never been over kind, but I chalked that up to his bad hand. It was near useless now, and the pain must have been horrible. Back in May, when I'd first come, he used to ask about my folks. Sometimes, he'd share stories about his little boy, Paul. Now he glanced over that pointed little nose and frowned sourly.

"Yu dink I don't know, Red Cap, but I do," he said one morning. It should have prepared me for the storm he cast my way, but it didn't. Wirz marched inside the orderly room and kicked Cable's drum across the room. He knocked a stack of books off their shelf, then stomped over to my desk and pounded his good hand on the letters I was writing, spilling ink over everything.

"Ees dees yur hand, Red Cap?" he screamed, digging a piece of paper from his pocket and mashing it against my face. I took the paper and stepped back. Opening it up, I recognized one of the maps Cable and I had supplied the escaping prisoners.

"Vas found vit a man ve captured in Macon. Ees dees yur hand? Ja, it ees."

I nodded and returned the map to him.

"Yu don't lie even? Vat ees dees yu do? I trust yu, leave yu to svim ven yu should verk, to go to town? Ja, I let maybe de ladies take yu in, feed yu cake! Yu I treat like my own dear Paul, and yu all de time make maps fur de Yankees."

"I'm a Yankee myself," I told him. "A Union soldier. How could I do otherwise?"

He grabbed me by the collar with his good hand and lifted me in the air. Shaking me, he screamed. As always when he got overexcited, he fell back on his German. He shook me harder, and I worried he might sling me right

125

through a window. Cable hollered, and a pair of Georgia reserves ran in, saw what was happening, and restrained the captain.

"Ja, yu lie to me, Red Cap. Yu, get him from mein sight, dees little liar! I should hang him, ja? Should cut out hees ungrateful heart and feed it to de dogs!"

I shuddered at the notion. Staring into those dark eyes, I deemed it possible.

"Now!" Wirz screamed. "Drow him in vit de odders, Corporal. See how yu like dat, Red Cap!"

The Georgians stacked their rifles and dragged me from the orderly room.

"R. J.?" Cable called, starting after me. Wirz barred his exit, though, and I hoped he wouldn't own up to making maps himself. Was no use both of us ending up inside.

"There now, boy, you've gone and got the captain stirred up something awful," the Georgia corporal said when he released his grip on my arm. His companion did likewise. "If'n I was you, I'd find a place to lay low."

They nudged me through the open gate and past the guards. I'd made a hundred trips into the compound, but this one was different. Not since the rebs had stolen my clothes back in Staunton had I felt so naked and vulnerable. Even then Red was at my side. I was alone this time.

I stumbled around the prison for half an hour.

"What news you bring us, Red Cap?" a man called.

"Got a spare carrot, son?" another asked.

"Ten dollars for an onion. Got one, Red Cap?"

I shook my head and stumbled along. Finally I drifted to the shebang Johnny Poland shared with Privates Bearer and Hushman. Daner was at the hospital now, and all of us knew that meant he was as good as dead.

126

"R. J., I warned you to stay away," Poland barked when I sat down beside him.

"Where else would I go?" I asked, fighting the urge to cry. "Wirz's thrown me in here for good."

"Got tired of his pet, did he?" a newcomer asked, laughing.

Poland, weak as he was, stepped over and flattened the man.

"Won't abide such talk," Poland announced. "He's scarce fifteen, and small to boot, but he's never in his life proved less than a man. Ain't a man in Company I wouldn't soldier with him any day."

"Not much left of Company I," Hushman observed. "But the three of us'll dust off anybody to say otherwise."

I believe they would have taken on the other thirty thousand that moment, and it cheered me. The Illinois cavalrymen from up the way drifted over to offer me a cup of good water from their well, and I found myself invited to a hundred different messes.

"Don't you worry, son," a batch of West Virginia newcomers told me. "Ain't a day somebody hereabouts ain't shared a Red Cap tale. You been a brightness at midnight."

It was a warming notion.

The trouble was, we didn't need anything to warm us that August. Once the dust settled at the orderly room, Cable escaped long enough to bring my few belongings over.

"Wish I could offer some food," he said, "but it cost me my dinner to get those Georgians there to let me inside. Wirz has issued orders against it."

"Then you best hurry back," I said, dropping my chin. "No good you being in here, too."

"Was my map."

"No, it was one I copied. Cable, you look after yourself."

"I will," he promised. "Do the same. You know the captain's brought in four new boys to do your work. He's cussing 'em already. Bet he'll ask you back."

His eyes told me otherwise, and I knew in my heart it wouldn't happen. I was in the stockade until I was exchanged—or dead.

14

Being on the outside of those tall pine logs, I'd never imagined the horrors of life on the inside. I now got a quick education in the realities of living—and dying—Andersonville-style. Back in February rations had always included meat, and the meal, though coarse, was generally edible. Most times there were some peas and beans, occasionally a potato and carrot. By summer, prisoners went whole weeks without meat, and what there was generally had spoiled. Armies of weevils infested the cornmeal, and the rebs had yet to grind it without putting in the husks. As a result many of the sicker boys cried out in agony as the hard kernels worked their way through their tormented innards.

I began to lose weight right away. I didn't notice it so much as others did. Johnny Poland offered to put an extra stitch or two in my trousers, seeing as they were a bit more generous than needed. And Bearer, whom I hardly knew, insisted on my accepting an extra share of our ration.

"You look to need it worse than me," I told him. "I've still got an inch or two covering my ribs."

"You're growin', son," he scolded. "Bad enough you should be in this place. A boy oughtn't to know want."

"Take it, R. J.," Poland urged. "Ain't the rest of us needin' food much longer."

I knew that as well as anyone, but I couldn't accept such sacrifices. I was closing in on five feet, and I meant more than ever to carry myself as a man.

Then, on August 9, old Poland shooed the rest of our boys off and made me sit beside him on his blanket.

"Ranny Powell," he said, gripping my shoulders with what feeble strength remained, "I got words just for you this night."

"You've never called me that before," I said, drawing back.

"Danny Hays did, and it never failed to bring on a smile. I figured to need one this night."

"We could all use one of Danny's pranks."

"I got no children to carry on my name," he said, shivering at the sound of the words. "Ain't got nothin' to leave 'em anyhow. Just this."

He dug under his blanket and produced a small canvas sack. Inside were a dozen brass buttons he'd earned working for the Illinois laundry, two silver dollars, and a wrinkled photograph of himself taken in muster camp back in '62.

"I'd have you save the picture as a keepsake, son," he mumbled. "Swap the buttons with them Georgia guards for what you need. I will 'em to you, together with this fine shebang you and Red Armhult started way back when. We moved it and improved it some, but it's yours just the same. I spoke with that batch from the Fourteenth West Virginia, over past the Illinois boys' well. Be a pack of them joining you when Bearer and Hushman pass. They're next sure."

"Don't talk that way!" I yelled.

"You figure we want it more'n you do?" he asked, laughing as tears ran down his face. "I'm hungry to see the green fields of home, Ranny, but I'll die here and be laid out by the gate 'fore mornin'. Son, I got no feelin' past my waist, and it's the same way Sam Brooks was 'fore he went. Scurvy's got me in a stranglehold, and ain't likely he'll let up now."

"I'll sit up with you. We'll get you some broth."

"Be wasted on me," he said, placing the canvas bag in my hands. "Remember me sometimes, Red Cap." He stared up at the ridiculous kepi and laughed. "Grow tall and hard. There's need. I'm feared what's comin's worse'n what's behind us."

He rested his head back and seemed to breathe easier. His chest rose, stretching the pallid skin until it fell again. Then it failed to rise, and I felt the fingers release their grip on my hand.

"Poland?" I called. "Johnny?"

He didn't answer. Andersonville had claimed another good man.

We put him out with the long line of the dead that next morning, and I guarded the body myself lest someone try to steal his clothes. I would have accompanied him to the trench and sung him a hymn, but the guards recognized me and blocked the way.

"Cap'n would skin us if we was to let you loose, Red Cap," one told me. "He ain't quit screamin' yet!"

Two weeks later when Bearer gave up the ghost, they were more obliging. I sang for Bearer, for Johnny Poland, and for old Daner, who was brought out from the hospital, dead of typhus.

"Just you and me," Hushman observed when I returned to the shebang.

"Yeah, it's grown lonely," I told him.

"Be just you 'fore much longer," he added. "Then nobody at all."

It seemed to me the rebs were hurrying us toward that end. Poor Hushman couldn't even get to his feet, and I fetched his rations now. Together we got a loaf of cornbread—a brick it was called. We'd try to eat our half bricks a bit at a time, but they were always gone by noon, and we hungered the rest of the day. Anybody in Andersonville more than a month looked hungry all the time, and I walked around cautiously.

"There's men here envious of the flesh still on you," Hushman warned. "A little sailor boy over a ways up and disappeared. When they found his body he was shy a leg."

I shuddered, and he grinned. I never knew if Hushman was telling the truth or not. Just the same I stayed away from that batch of shebangs.

The sailors among us were an odd lot. Some of those rough old men sort of adopted the ships' boys, tended 'em almost like sweethearts. It was something to see those "barnacle backs," as Hush called them, tending some poor child. One boy, who was near as fine a thief as ole Mosby the raider, got himself caught and bashed proper. A giant of a sailor tended him in his dying days, and when the boy died, the giant didn't live out the week.

The other oddities among us were the Negroes. At first the rebs mostly sent those they captured to work on fortifications. When the federal government found out, they pulled some southern boys out and put them to like toil.

Now those poor black-skinned fellows suffered like the rest of us—or worse. They weren't used to idleness, and it worked on them cruelly. They also had no resistance to disease, and fevers swept off whole companies of them.

The sole heartening news we had that terrible August was that Sherman was moving steadily on Atlanta. Grant was after Richmond from the south now, we learned, fighting Bob Lee at Petersburg. Now that confused me, for I remembered the Petersburg in the Shenandoah Valley.

"There's a town named that south of Richmond, too," Hush explained. "It's where we switched trains. Remember?"

I could barely recall yesterday, much less a February train ride.

The last days of August a storm blew in, and it washed the camp with a fierce downpour.

"The answer to our prayers," the Illinois boys claimed. Before you knew it everyone in the camp was standing out under the rain, stripping himself naked, and screaming out thanks to the Almighty. It was heartrending to see thirty thousand scarecrows jumping around, counting one another's ribs. It was a sad day for the graybacks, too, for many a louse got itself washed out past Sweetwater Branch. As for that accursed stream, runoff surged along, sweeping the mess from the sinks past the stockade. In fact one section of the log fence gave way, and two Georgians were carried along when their roosts went floating along in the torrent.

Nights were downright pleasant for a time after the rain. It was cooler, and there was a sweetness to the air. It was days before the foul odor returned, and we found ourselves singing and carrying on like children having birthdays.

Most nights I stared at the stars and tried to bring back to me my father's wise words. I could barely recall his face. Ma seemed a world away, too. Strange how I could always hear their voices in my dreams, though.

The guard posts sang out every half hour in a sort of melodic chant, and you got so you could recognize who had the watch. Those we didn't know by name picked up nicknames.

"Nine o'clock and all's well!" a high-pitched voice would yell.

"That's Bare-kneed Homer," Hush would say, rolling over beside me. "Ain't got his britches patched yet, that boy."

There were others less likely to bring on a smile. Dead-eye Danley had shot three men near the deadline. He'd missed his target each time and dropped an innocent sitting in a shebang. We were a mass of people, and a shot was bound to find a mark.

One night the first week of September the guards were hollering out like always.

"Eight o'clock and all's well," made the rounds.

"Half past eight and all's well," started around the wall. About halfway, though, some poor fellow in an agitated voice shouted, "Half past eight and Atlanta's gone to hell!"

A cheer rose from three corners of the prison and merged in the middle. North of Sweetwater Branch the boys took up singing "The Star Spangled Banner." South of the stream it was "Rally Round the Flag." Men near dead revived long enough to toss their hats and rejoice.

"How far's Atlanta from Andersonville?" Hush asked me when I returned to the shebang after sharing a cup of well water with the Illinois cavalry.

"Half the state away," I answered.

"Well," Hush said, gazing north, "at least I lived to see Atlanta fall."

He lay down then, and I read death in his eyes. Was like that sometimes. Men could revive so you figured them hale and hearty. Then they'd give up.

Next morning Billy Sturgiss came to share our shebang. He was one of the boys from the Fourteenth, tall and long legged, fair of complexion, with red hair and gray eyes that reminded me of Red Armhult. He was a drummer, too, though he was past twenty.

"Fool that I was, I was near through college," he told me. "Had real schooling. If I'd known the war would last, I could have waited and finished. They would have made me a general. Well, an officer anyway. I proved I was fool enough to be a colonel just leaving school like I did."

Billy cheered me up, and he even managed to bring out a smile on Hushman's sunken cheeks. We neither one of us had a drum, but that didn't hinder Billy. He got some canvas and wrapped it around both ends of a barrel with the top and bottom cut out. It sounded more like a tom-tom than a snare drum, but we nevertheless beat up a storm. And we'd pass the evenings singing and cheering our neighbors.

Billy was downright clever. He'd take a song and change the words. Instead of singing about John Brown's body, we'd find ourselves wailing away about Bob Lee's drawers. My favorite ones were about ole Grant. He wasn't the most popular fellow around, not with a fair chunk of the boys taken in the Wilderness and at Spotsylvania. New arrivals told of the bloody charges at Cold Harbor, where the rebs shot up a whole division in an hour and never lost an inch of ground. It was Fredericksburg all over again.

Rumors of a new exchange flew through the prison. A second rumor said Sherman was hurrying down from Atlanta to free us. I didn't see what could stop him myself.

135

Here were thirty thousand soldiers awaiting liberty, and him only days away. In the end, though, it was fresh rebs who arrived.

"We'll all be dead before winter," Hush grumbled.

"Somebody'll be coming any day," I argued.

"Nobody cares, R. J.," Hush said. "Beat your drum for me when they drop me in the trench, will you?"

He died the next day.

I could have stood Hush's dying better if the rebs hadn't ordered a batch of us rounded up and freighted north that same day. It was September 6, and for the first time prisoners were headed out of Camp Sumter alive.

15

I was beating the drum for Hush around midday September 7 when a voice called to me from the road. I glanced up in time to see Cable Jackson marching with the latest batch to be sent north. He still had his drum slung over his shoulder, and if he appeared thinner than I recalled, he was in high spirits. I wished him well on his journey back to Pennsylvania.

I had grimmer work at hand. As I beat taps, I realized that of the twenty members of Company I to arrive seven months before, I alone had survived. I knew they'd often sacrificed that I might eat better. They'd shielded me from the scourge of raiders. They had worked on the Illinois well so I could drink untainted water.

And there was Lewis Jones, too. I recalled his grin, the way he eased his rifle into my hands so I could shoot that deer. He'd saved my life sure as if he'd fished me, drowning, from a river.

"Boy, you all right?" a guard asked as I closed my eyes and recalled the many faces of the friends who lay buried in that

Georgia clay. Red Armhult. Sam Brooks. Jimmy Dyer. Old Poland.

"Red Cap, we got to get you back inside," another guard said, nudging my elbow with the flat of his bayonet. "Come on, boy, don't make me hit you. I ain't got the heart."

I blinked my eyes open and stared into the face of a stubble-bearded sergeant not any older than Billy Sturgiss. I nodded and followed the ragged wretches who'd carried the dead to their rest.

Back in the stockade rumors were rife. We were being rescued or exchanged. Grant had taken Richmond. A peace treaty had been signed. The British were invading from Canada! I only laughed and returned to my shebang.

"Here's your drum, Billy," I said, setting it down. "Wasn't so good as I hoped, but I got it done."

"Maybe you should keep it," he told me. His usual grin was gone, and I touched my hand to his forehead. He was on fire.

"We'll get you to the hospital," I announced. "I'll fetch a surgeon."

"Want me dead so fast?" he asked. "The fever will pass, R. J. It's scurvy I'll die of."

"We're almost free," I argued. "I'll talk to the guards, see if you can't go north with the next batch."

"They won't take anybody who's sick. And I'd never make the trip, shut up in a boxcar and all."

"Then we'll get you well," I promised. "Scurvy can be battled. I'll get you some vegetables, fruit . . ."

"R. J., don't get yourself all lathered."

"Soap. I'll get you scrubbed."

He shook his head and laughed, but I was serious. I grabbed my pouch of buttons and set off to do business with the Georgia reserve. By nightfall I had two onions, a handful of beans, and a juicy Florida orange. I got them all down Billy, and the next day I traded near everything in the shebang—even our iron kettle—for some turnips. They seemed to ease his sufferings some, but when I took him over to the Illinois boys, and we stripped him so we could do a proper washing, I saw how well he'd hidden his plight. His ankles were swollen past recognition, and his knees were rigid. His chest was caved in. Teeth were loose, and his hair was coming out in places.

"Don't you go and die on me, Billy Sturgiss!" I shouted as the cavalrymen washed a crust of filth from him. "We got songs to make up."

"Won't be 'When Billy Comes Marchin' Home,' " he declared.

Three reb guards came to fetch me on the tenth.

"Seems there's a whole regiment swears it won't leave till you go, Red Cap," one of them told me. I knew better, of course. It was either the guards, or else Wirz had forgiven me. Either way, I shook my head.

"I can't go," I told them. "Billy's sick."

"We'll see him tended," the boys of the Fourteenth promised.

"Ain't that boy gettin' out of Georgia, Red Cap," one told me matter-of-factly.

"Then I aim to wait it out with him," I explained. "He'd do the same for me."

"Likely you're right," a sorrowful sergeant admitted. "Billy's got heart, if little sense. Do you know they caught him stragglin'? Could've got clean away but he wouldn't leave his fool drum behind. They took it from him anyway, of course, but that's Billy."

139

I asked him later if that was true, and he laughed.

"As I remember it, I dropped the drum and lit out for open country," he whispered. "Reb cavalry cut me off, though. I do like the other version of the tale better."

That night I swapped a little reb my boots and jacket for a pear. I ended up sharing it with the Illinois boys, though, because Billy couldn't swallow. His eyes had gotten almost yellow, and he asked me to fetch a pen. He couldn't write because his fingers were stiff and swollen, but he told me what to put down, and I wrote three letters. There was one to his folks, a second to a girl back home in Preston County, and the last one was to a young cousin. His words were full of quiet comfort and good humor. I hoped when my turn came I'd have the courage to think of others like that.

Billy lasted through the thirteenth. That night he sort of melted away in the darkness. I carried him to the gate myself. He was near a foot taller, but he weighed less than a hundred pounds. I was but seventy or so myself—maybe less from starving, but I wouldn't let anybody else touch him. Later, after beating taps, I laid his drum in the trench beside him.

The rebs were lining up a fresh group to send north when the guards marched me back to the stockade. Suddenly somebody shouted, "Make way for Red Cap!" The sea of men parted like I was Moses. One of the Illinois boys grabbed my shoulders and turned me toward the front of the group.

"It's not my turn," I argued.

"Sure, it is," somebody claimed, and I was shuffled along by dozens of hands.

"Name?" a reb lieutenant asked.

"Red . . . Ransom J. Powell," I told him. "Tenth West Virginia Volunteer Infantry."

"How old are you, boy?" he asked, scratching his head.

"Fifteen," I answered.

"And growin'," somebody behind me added.

"Hope you get back home, youngster," the lieutenant whispered.

Moments later I marched out at the head of five hundred walking skeletons. "The Camp Sumter cadavers," the reb surgeon dubbed us. I was halfway to Macon before I found out what that meant. It's a dead body!

Well, we weren't all of us dead. And even the sickest among us was full of hope. We dreamed of freedom, of being exchanged, of furloughs home and pockets full of back pay.

I bit my lip and tried to revive the sorrow I felt for Billy. But the motion of the boxcar shook all the sadness out of me. Prospects were too fair to allow gloom to edge its way back into my being. I took up the words of "Bob Lee's Drawers" and honored Billy's best side. The whole car cheered, and by the time we reached Savannah, the entire train knew that song!

Savannah was a blur. The heat and confinement brought on a fever. Together with most of my companions, I was marched along the tracks to a sort of hospital. Our hair was cut, and we were given a good scrubbing by a batch of rough-handed Negro women who eyed us with suspicion and muttered prayers when they discovered our wasted state.

They seemed to enjoy the younger ones, though. Me they delighted in poking and tickling. I welcomed the warm lather, but I wasn't used to being bathed by females, and I reddened with embarrassment when they teased me about being a shrunk Yankee.

"I seen some rebs no bigger," I complained.

"Dey musta been li'l babies," a girl answered, laughing.

Bathed and revived, I was examined by a doctor who noted my fever and ordered me confined in bed till it passed. Fortunately the food wasn't bad there. Mostly I had mush in the morning and a vegetable soup in the afternoon. If it was scurvy tormenting me, the carrots and peas were sure to give it a fight.

"Have you had fever before?" a doc asked two days later.

"Had a battle with tertian fever back in '63," I explained.

"Camp Sumter was good treatment for that!" he said, scowling. "You may have out-and-out malaria. Or it might just be intermittent fever. If it's malaria, you'll be here a while. If it passes, we'll ship you along to Charleston."

"Where's the exchange to be made?" I asked.

"I've heard of no exchange," he answered. "Only that Georgia is too hot for prisons just now."

He wasn't talking temperature, I knew. Sherman had brought us out of Andersonville. But as for the future, a stockade in Charleston, which was well known as a Yankee-hating town, didn't make for a pleasant prospect.

I was relieved when the fever broke, for malaria and yellow fever were well-documented southern nightmares. My intermittent fever would return, the doctor told me, but I was well enough to be moved to Charleston. They shipped me north the last part of September, where I stayed in a tobacco warehouse near a rail station.

By then rumors of exchange were wasted on us. Too many disappointments had tormented us, and we wouldn't bite that hook again. The first week of October a group of reb officers arrived with two preachers, though, and they began sifting through us in search of sailors.

142

"It's been agreed," they explained, "to exchange naval prisoners immediately."

"You just became a sailor, Red Cap," a big seaman from Baltimore told me. "Now listen good so if they ask you, you have the story down pat."

"I'm not a sailor," I argued. "I won't—"

"Look, boy, we're tired of your fool songs," a tall sergeant declared.

"Don't listen to them," the sailor grumbled. "It's not that at all. You done us favors, bringin' word of the war, passin' on maps and such. We all know why ole Wirz threw you back inside, and I'll be hanged if you spend one hour longer locked up in this hole than I can help."

By the time the rebs got to me, I'd become Walter Parsons, a second class boy off the steamer *Southfield*, sunk in Albemarle Sound by the reb ram that trapped the poor Plymouth pilgrims. I wasn't the only boy to be likewise substituted. For every powder monkey or deckhand buried at Andersonville or drowned in Albemarle Sound, some young soldier or other was put in his place. I worried that if lists were made my own name's absence might worry my family, but the sailors said no one was going to wade through the names of forty-five thousand soldiers sent to Georgia looking for what wasn't there.

The second week of October, barefoot and with only a tattered blanket over a pair of worn trousers and a frayed shirt, I rode in a rickety boxcar northward. On October 16, together with a small group of other naval prisoners, I was handed over by the rebs to a waiting escort of dandy-dressed bluecoats.

"Lord, they've starved them to bones," the colonel in charge gasped. Then he instructed us to climb aboard

143

wagons, and we were taken to the little town of Varina, Virginia. A clerk recorded our names, and we were put aboard a steamer at City Point, the supply depot for Grant's army even then hammering away at the rebs guarding Petersburg.

As we sailed past a Massachusetts regiment newly arrived on the field, we received a hearty cheer.

"Hurrah for the poor devils from Andersonville!" the shout went. And it continued for miles as we chugged along the James River and on toward home.

16

Our ship docked at a small pier in the harbor of Annapolis, Maryland. The officers in charge of our pitiful little company announced we had arrived at Camp Parole. The sailors recognized the place as the old naval academy, lately moved north and away from the unwelcome attentions of the southern armies.

Those able to walk were paraded to a nearby building. The disabled were helped along by soldiers. Once inside, we boys were nudged to the front. I was third in line and taken in hand by a white-coated hospital attendant.

"Feet don't look too good," he observed as he snatched away my rags, leaving me standing there like a plucked chicken. He lifted my arms and examined the army of graybacks burrowed in my armpits and in my scalp. "Got more lice here than Grant's got soldiers," the man said, laughing. He turned me around, poked my belly some, had me bend my joints. Then, while a group of boys with pitchforks flung my rags over a railing and into the beds of wagons, he started me toward the next room.

"Wait," he then called. "Toss the cap there, sonny."

"No," I answered. "I had it all the time I was a prisoner."

"Sure, and there's as many lice in it as on you, I expect. Toss it."

I gazed around in search of someone to argue with, but the others were busy with my companions. Standing naked save for a crust of grit, I wouldn't have been very convincing anyhow. The attendant snatched my cap and tossed it toward the railing. It was scooped up and forked—gone.

"Come along with you," another attendant urged. I stumbled onward until he gripped me firmly and set me on a stool. Then, taking out some shears, he hacked away my hair till there was nothing but stubble left. Even that was too much, though. He made a lather of shaving soap and razored me bald.

"Don't feel so bad," he said, helping me up. "I've shaved men of beards they've been half a lifetime growing. Only way to rid 'em of the lice."

For once I was glad to be late growing whiskers.

The third room we entered was full of great wooden tubs. Two fellows grabbed me and deposited me in a tub. Half a foot of soap suds swam on the surface, and the men took to scrubbing me with sponges. I couldn't see what they were doing to me, but across the way they were rubbing two layers of skin off another boy.

Once they contented themselves I was as clean as humanly possible, they lifted me from the tub and turned me over to another pair. These men applied huge cotton towels to me. It wasn't enough I should be dry. They rubbed half the starch from my bones. My eyes burned with traces of a white powder they peppered me with, and a doctor came over and painted my raw feet with iodine.

"I've had a touch of fever," I whispered.

"I'd be startled to hear otherwise, youngster," he answered with a grin. "You'll have more if you don't run along and let them find you some clothes."

Isn't my notion to be standing here naked, I thought to say. But then I was only one of the dozens being run through that hospital gauntlet. After Andersonville it was hard to feel abused by a little soap and water.

I waddled along to the clothing room. Quartermasters were issuing drawers, socks, pantaloons, and blue jumpers. They gave me slippers and a hospital gown, too. It was real sport, finding the right sizes for everyone, and I was glad to be one of the first. They weren't expecting so many boys, nor men so whittled down in size.

I wasted no time getting into my new clothes. It felt wondrous fine, to be clean and warm after so many months of neglect. I stepped up to a long table, and a corporal asked me all sorts of information.

"Name?" he inquired.

"Ransom J. Powell," I answered.

"Powell? Ain't got no Powell on my list," he grumbled. "Ship?"

I stared blankly.

"You an idiot, boy? What ship were you aboard? What's your rank? Where were you captured? When and where were you released?"

I sighed. Then I told them the tale of not really being Walter Parsons of the steamer *Southfield*, of how I'd been persuaded to adopt a dead boy's name and escape confinement alive.

The corporal slammed a fist down on the table and rushed off to fetch an officer. Next thing I knew two soldiers with rifles were leading me to a small side room. In half an hour the room was near full of us. A white-haired colonel stormed in, cursing rebel deceit and complaining about lying boys.

"You boys may well have put an end to the exchange," he scolded. "Such trickery is why the cartel broke down."

We all turned pale. The colonel stormed and strutted.

"I guess you best send us back, Colonel," one of the boys suggested. "We ain't any of us come here to do the cause an injustice."

"Send us back," a second and a third argued. "We got a good wash. It'll get us through Christmas."

The soldiers assigned to guard us turned toward that colonel with murder in their eyes. I knew what the others must have suspected. Those soldiers wouldn't let anybody send us anywhere! We were thin as rails and pitifully small.

"Well, get their correct names and units," the colonel finally ordered. "And see they're outfitted correctly. I won't have infantry wearing those fool sailor suits."

We raised a cheer. In no time we were led back to the tables and told to identify ourselves correctly. I watched in dismay as the corporal made note of my assuming a false name to effect an early exchange. It was the only blot on my military record, and it galled me. They might have overlooked the whole thing considering my months of suffering.

"Ain't like an army to forget, though," a boy named Hank Clinton, who was also from Maryland, told me when the attendants escorted us to a small room with two identical

148

metal beds. I could smell the freshness of the linens, and neither Hank nor I wasted any time shucking our robes and piling into our beds.

A surgeon paid us a call shortly. He asked a thousand questions, scratching notes on a card which he then placed in a tin holder on our beds. He seemed pleased at my tongue and teeth, frowned a bit when he noticed my ribs protruding, and worried over my ankles some.

"Guess we'll live, eh?" I asked Hank after the doctor left.

"Never considered elsewise," he replied cheerfully.

Our next visitor was a tall sergeant, chief of the dining room. He brought along a little fellow with a notebook, and they jotted down notes from our cards.

"Special diet," he told us. I frowned, but Hank immediately asked what sort of special diet.

"Double rations," the clerk said, grinning. "And all the cocoa you can drink."

True to their word they brought trays of ham steak, boiled potatoes, carrots, and wheat rolls. I thought myself dead and gone to heaven. And that night, sleeping peacefully on the soft feather mattress, I wasn't sure I wanted to wake.

The next morning they looked us over again. Content we were sure to live a while, we were escorted to the paymaster, who doled out two months pay—twenty-six dollars for privates and drummers—plus twenty-five cents a day ration money for every day we'd been prisoners. I wound up with close to a hundred twenty dollars, a small fortune. The same colonel who had chastised us for using false names then issued us thirty-day furloughs.

"Upon expiration, report to the nearest camp of rendezvous," he instructed us. Those like me, bound for western Maryland, were given directions to the B & O depot.

"I'm off for Baltimore," Hank said as we shook hands at the station. "Good luck to you, Ransom Powell."

"Good luck to you," I said, waving him toward his train. An hour later I climbed into a fourth-class carriage headed for Cumberland. Bound for home. At least for a month the war was behind me.

Epilogue

FOR RANSOM POWELL, the war was, indeed, over. Hardly was he home when the fever that plagued him in Savannah returned. On November 14, 1864, just days before his furlough expired, he was examined by surgeons at the U.S. General Hospital in Cumberland, Maryland, where he had gone to catch the Baltimore and Ohio express back to Annapolis where he would go by steamer back to the Tenth West Virginia, now surrounding Petersburg.

"Sick with intermittent fever," the doctors recorded on his military records. "Unable to travel."

While Robert E. Lee and Ulysses S. Grant fought their desperate battle south of Richmond, the campaign that led in April 1865 to Lee's surrender at Appomattox, R. J. Powell lay feverish in the hospital first at Cumberland and later at Claysville, a step closer to his home in Frostburg. Intermittent fever was but one legacy of Andersonville to plague him.

After the war, young Powell labored for a time in the mines of western Maryland. He fell in love with Maggie Watson, and in 1870 they were married in Washington

Hollow, Allegheny County, Maryland. Afterward R. J. went to work as a clerk in the federal pension office, where his fine penmanship and concern for his fellow veterans made him many friends.

Shortly after John McElroy, one of the Illinois cavalrymen Powell was to remember with fondness, published his memoir of life in Andersonville with its moving account of the boy known as "Little Red Cap," R. J. contacted the author. In later editions of McElroy's book, a note was included identifying Red Cap to his many admirers. Powell and McElroy corresponded regularly afterward.

In later years, R. J. Powell proved to be a great letter writer and entertaining tale-spinner. While swapping war stories with General Rufus Dawes in 1894, Powell learned of a rare gesture of goodwill made by the governor of Alabama, Thomas Goode Jones. Governor Jones had returned to the state of Ohio several regimental flags captured in the war and spoke of putting aside differences and mending old wounds. Powell, suspecting that perhaps this might be the same Lieutenant Jones whose younger brother had befriended a small boy in a southern prison camp, wrote the governor a moving letter, which survives to this day—a testament to the courage of a fifteen-year-old boy and the humanity of a Confederate private.

Marietta Ohio Sept. 30, 1894

To His Excellency.
The Governor of Alabama.

Dear Sir:

During the War of the Rebellion in January 1864 I was taken a prisoner of war and about Feb. 1864 I was taken to

Andersonville. Lewis Jones, a Private of the 26 Ala. secured permission to take me on the outside of the prison on condition that I would beat the drum for the 26 Ala. on "guard mount" Dress Parade &c while they would remain at Andersonville on duty. Mr. Jones took me to the camp of the 26 Ala. and explained to me the conditions in which I would be put on "Parole of Honor" and given certain liberties. I refused to accept the conditions and Lewis Jones gave me something to eat and put me back in the stockade explaining to me that he had no authority to keep me out only on the conditions to which I have referred. They soon succeeded in getting a good drummer and fifer out of the stockade that did the work I refused to do. I was a small boy having enlisted when I was four feet in height and only thirteen years of age. In a short time Lewis Jones came to the stockade and took me out and made another proposition to me. He said he had secured permission to take me out of the stockade and that he was responsible for my safe-keeping.

He took me to the camp of the 26 Ala. and I slept and ate with him, and he took me hunting and fishing a time or two. I do not recollect his company, but there were five in his mess and I made six. We ate together, and I had nothing to do but behave myself and not run away. He was very kind to me and said he interested himself in my behalf on account of me being a mere child and that seeing me a prisoner of war had aroused the tender feelings of his heart.

In that mess of six was a brother of Lewis Jones who was a Lieut. in the company to which Lewis belonged. In a few weeks the 26 Ala. was ordered into active service and during all the time until they took their departure I staid in camp with Lewis Jones and he treated me, and cared for me, as if I were his own child. Before they left he went to

Captain Wirz, the commandant of the Prison, and arranged for him to keep me at his office and run errands, and not put me back in the stockade. I staid with Captain Wirz a good while, but one day he flew into a rage and put me into the stockade.

When I tell you that I went into Andersonville with nineteen of my company and I was the only one that reached home alive you will readily see how Lewis Jones saved my life. The better treatment at Wirz's office and the kind treatment from Lewis Jones, and it was all due to the efforts of Lewis Jones, built me up in health so that I was able to live through it. LEWIS JONES SAVED MY LIFE.

When you were in Marietta, Ohio, a few years ago, returning a flag, you were at the home of Gen'l Rufus R. Dawes of that city. I was relating this incident to Gen'l Dawes recently and he said it would not surprise him to learn that the Lieut. Jones to whom I have referred was none other than the present Governor of the State of Alabama, and he urged me to write you a letter to ascertain if you are Lieut. Jones of the 26 Ala. and where my friend Lewis Jones can be located. I have never seen or heard of Lewis Jones since he waved good bye to me on the cars at Andersonville Station. He may be in Heaven long ago for no other place would be fitted for his generous soul. Although I have always intended to try to locate him this is the first effort that I have made in that direction. Do me the kindness to favor me with a reply and I will highly appreciate it. I am 45 years of age and I was a Private and Drummer in Company "I" 10th W. Va. Vol. Inft.

Very truly yours, R. J. Powell

We don't know whether R. J. Powell ever received an answer to his letter. We do know, however, that Governor Thomas Goode Jones was not Lewis Jones's brother.

Four and a half years later, on January 24, 1899, Ransom J. Powell died in Marietta, Ohio, as a result of chronic asthma, acquired during months of privation at Andersonville. He left behind his wife of twenty-nine years, Maggie; five children; and the memory of faith, love, duty, and uncompromising spirit.

Lewis Jones survived Hood's bloody Tennessee campaign, but nothing is known of his later years.

Captain Henry Wirz was tried, sentenced, and hanged for the evils of Andersonville. Today many historians consider him a scapegoat for incompetent management and impossible supply problems. Nowhere is there evidence of Andersonville prisoners protesting his wrongful death, though. Justly or not, Wirz was the focus of the survivors' hatred.

Author's Note

ANDERSONVILLE served as home to some forty-five thousand Union prisoners during its fourteen-month existence. Almost thirteen thousand of those men and boys died there. How many others had their lives shortened can never be known. If Andersonville had been a battle, it would have been the most costly engagement of the war for the North.

Were the horrors of the place the result of Confederate determination to kill its prisoners? Were conditions there worse than at Union camps like Elmira, New York, or Camp Douglas, Illinois? Only in size and magnitude of suffering was Andersonville unique. Civil War prisons as a whole were nightmarish. Fifty-five thousand soldiers, Northern and Southern, died in confinement.

In 1863 no one on earth had ever held large numbers of prisoners. The custom was to award captives a parole following combat. They would simply promise not to fight anymore and go home. In the early days of the Civil War, men were made to pledge not to fight until "properly exchanged." In the muddled way things were done, a cartel was formed that oversaw these exchanges. Soon, though, errors were made. Suspicions grew. And General U. S. Grant, believing the exchange would lead to prolonged Southern resistance, ordered it terminated. In doing so for the right reasons, he doomed the Andersonville thousands and others elsewhere to the worst sort of fate. Whether more died in prison than would have been slain had the war continued another year or more will never be known. If not, then perhaps Grant should be praised for his courageous decision. At the time, though, he was attacked by the families of prisoners and cursed by the prisoners themselves.

Following the war, only the prisoners' graveyard was preserved at Andersonville. The stockade collapsed, and pines reclaimed the interior. People wanted to forget the horror.

Today, at the Andersonville National Historic Site, the slow process of rebuilding the stockade commences. In summer, park rangers create living history. There also stands a prisoner of war museum with exhibits witnessing other horrors of a more recent vintage. It's said that when we forget history, we are doomed to repeat it.

Red Cap is not intended as a testament to nightmare. Rather I hope it will bear witness to how the human spirit can triumph over the greatest adversity. Often lost amid the better-known tales of Andersonville—the Raiders, the trigger-happy Georgia reserves—are the stories of the Georgians who reached out a helping hand to the prisoners, the slaves who smuggled food into the stockade, and the one Alabama private who chose compassion before cruelty and thus saved a small boy's life.

Acknowledgments

THIS BOOK has been seven years in the making. At times the search for "Red Cap" seemed at a dead end, but always some new trace of him would surface, and the chase would resume. I owe many debts, and I will try here to acknowledge a few of them.

A librarian friend, Margie Prater, first introduced me to John McElroy's work, and thus to Ransom Powell. To McElroy, Amos E. Stearns, John Ransom, and Ira Pettit, diarists all, I owe my knowledge of the events at Camp Sumter that fateful February to September 1864.

William E. Lind of the Military Reference Branch of the National Archives assisted in the search for R. J. Powell's military and pension files. His hints directed me to microfilm rolls, where I located the Powell family's census records for 1860 and learned of the campaigns and battles of the Tenth West Virginia. Further information was culled from the *Official Records of the War of the Rebellion*—the voluminous archive of the Civil War in which is found a detailed report of the battle at Droop Mountain and the other activities of the regiment.

To my father, Charles C. Wisler, Jr., who took time off while visiting Washington, D. C., to comb the National Archives and copy a shelf full of documents, and who ever since has shared my fascination with a fifteen-year-old Yankee drummer boy, I am equally indebted.

Mark Ragan, Park Ranger at the Andersonville National Historic Site, provided me with a copy of R. J. Powell's letter to the governor of Alabama. No one at Andersonville knows what happened after R. J. sent this letter, but reading Powell's story in his own words, in his own handwriting, spurred me on. Mark unfortunately was off battling forest fires when I visited the park in August 1989. To the park staff, who allowed me access to the historic files, and to the many volunteers who devoted time and energy to the 125th anniversary of Andersonville, I express my great thanks. To Terry Peake and Luther Terry, my Scouting friends who agreed to visiting the park on our way home from the National Boy Scout Jamboree, I owe the stark memory of strolling through rows of shebangs and climbing a ladder to a guard's roost.

Ranny Powell appeared as a touching character in MacKinlay Kantor's novel, *Andersonville*. This book brought new exposure to the prison, and its bibliography headed me toward many sources. My copy is a gift from my agent and friend Barbara Puechner.

Last, but far from least, I am grateful to the public libraries of Garland and Plano, Texas. I began my search in the former, and it was at the microfilm viewers of the latter that I unearthed many of the details that I hope bring realism and drama to these pages.

—G. Clifton Wisler
Plano, Texas

About the Author

Author G. CLIFTON WISLER says: "While working on a separate Andersonville project, I discovered an account of a young drummer boy named Ransom Powell. I became intrigued by this likable character who was offered a chance at refuge from war and privation—but who stuck to his promise to serve his country and cause."

An award-winning author, Mr. Wisler has written more than forty novels, many of them for young people. He lives in Plano, Texas.